STORIES OF THE END

Terry Pierson

Something Spooky

CONTENTS

Contents

SOMETHING IN
THE OCEAN

MIKE
How many times do we have to do this?

LIZARD
As many times as we need to.

SHAWN
I don't want to start anything. Just how I feel.

LIZARD
It's not about feelings. There are facts and lies. What
you are saying is simply not true.

KAREN
Can't we do something else? I get enough of this
out of every other moment of life.

The four friends are segregated into four little boxes. Each cozied into an equal percentage of the screen space, entrenched in their own small personal world which reaches beyond the borders of the picture, and holds lots of intimate details that the camera can never see.

They are twenty-something, only visible from the neckline up, primed and as well-lit as they could manage for people they see regularly. Each space shows little signs of their personality.

Mike's frame is aloof, as calm and neutral as he strives to be. His simple sweater vest, unremarkable features, and standard, medium-length hair-cut would make him impossible to describe to a sketch artist.

Lizard is as colorful as his name, strings of purple lights illuminate his background and cast a glow on his long, flowing hair. He is hunched over in front of the computer, leaning down to meet the camera at face level.

Shawn's setting is prim and proper, potted plants and a recently dusted bookshelf at a perfect depth of frame. He had lost a lot of weight since beginning treatment and his hair was starting to thin.

Karen's background is the same as for her stream, a carefully arranged bouquet explosion of video game merchandise and accessories. She's pretty but understated in appearance, baggy clothes and half interested glances while she works on another computer offscreen.

No one had said anything in a moment and everyone was starting to squirm uncomfortably.

                    KAREN
So, how about that new gameplay trailer, huh? Everybody see that?

There was a momentary pause. The kind of awkward silence that feels like a breath.

                    MIKE
Yeah, pretty cool. I'm still pumped.

                    LIZARD
It looks good but we didn't really learn anything new.

                    SHAWN
The climbing stuff looks cool. We don't get enough of that in games.

                    KAREN
Yeah, you'd think that would be more of a thing.

Lizard gets up and wanders into his background. There is a kitchen is-land, he grabs a bag of potato chips, and comes back into view.

SHAWN
Got the munchies?

LIZARD
What, because I eat I've got the munchies? But yes. Yes I do have
the munchies.Everyone laughs and the tension lifts.

MIKE
I think it's time I have another scotch.

LIZARD
Scotch, what a snob. Remember when we use to smash PBRs?

MIKE
Yes, I do. And you remind me every time I drink scotch.

LIZARD
That's because every time you drink scotch you talk
about drinking scotch like a real scotchy snob.

Mike is preparing his drink, wandering across the screen.

MIKE
Scotchy snob?

LIZARD
Yeah. Is that offensive? I didn't mean it offensively.

MIKE
I don't know if it's offensive but it's dumb.

SHAWN
Bathroom break, be right back.

His camera goes dark.

KAREN
Did you guys see the video of that thing that hit the ocean?

Mike, shaking the ice in his glass, sits back at his station.

MIKE
It "hit" the ocean?

KAREN
Well, it fell into the ocean. It crashed. Whatever.

MIKE
No, I haven't seen it. Just got online before this.

LIZARD
Yeah, I did. Pretty weird.

MIKE
What was it?

KAREN
I don't know, no one does. But there's this like grainy video
of this big thing falling from the sky and sinking.

MIKE
It sunk?

KAREN
I guess, I don't know. Here, I'll send the video.

She turns her full attention to the chat computer. Typing, the glow of the screen is reflected in her glasses.

LIZARD
Probably just a blimp or something.

He raises a glass bowl to his lips and scorches the green grass.

MIKE
I'm sorry, did you just say that a blimp sunk into the
ocean and nobody knows what happened?

Lizard exhales the smoke in huge clouds that filter his scene.

LIZARD
Not actually a blimp, obviously. But something normal
that people just haven't figured out yet.

Shawn's camera comes back on. He is right where he was, adjusting again to the contours of the chair.

                    KAREN
You just said that the video was pretty weird.

                    LIZARD
Well, it was weird! But it's still probably just something
            stupid no one has thought of yet.

                    KAREN
Whatever, here is the video. See for yourself.

The notification chime echoes through multiple speakers. Everyone directs their attention to the video.

                    KAREN
I mean, it seems pretty big to be a blimp...or whatever.

Mike's brow is furrowed, he is concentrating on the video, clicking to restart it and stroking his chin.

                    LIZARD
I don't think it's actually a blimp, just something that makes sense.

                    KAREN
                  Like a blimp?

                    LIZARD
                Shut up, Karen.

Shawn and Mike are still fixated on the footage. Finally, Mike relaxes his shoulders.

                    MIKE
I don't know. No idea. Probably something military.

                    SHAWN
              Could it be a satellite?

                    MIKE
              I don't think so. If-

The chat freezes. Everyone's square is locked. For an instant, the frames go dark, but no one knows who saw the same. Each assumes it was the connection.

Suddenly, they are all doing something different. None of them notice. Mike is eating. Lizard is doodling in a notebook. Shawn is combing through a folder of papers. Karen is sitting cross-legged, intent on the chat.

> LIZARD
> Anyway, I'm starving. I could go for some serious grub.

> SHAWN
> Got the munchies?

> MIKE
> You're a grown man. Cook something or order some food.

> LIZARD
> Yeah, I guess I should.

> KAREN
> Riveting conversation, y'all.

They all feel like they are acting normal.

> MIKE
> I think it's time I have another scotch.

Each of their rooms begin to fill with an unusual color, a sort of illuminated magenta.

> KAREN
> Uh guys, what is that?

> SHAWN
> Woah, what the hell?

> LIZARD
> You guys see that too?

They are looking around their rooms and to their cameras.

> MIKE
> It's each of us. It's everywhere?

> KAREN
> Is it outside?

> SHAWN
> No, I don't know where it is. I don't know where it is!

He jumps up and kicks his chair out. Rubbing his palms down his sweater, his shoulders spike in tension.

> SHAWN (cont'd)
> Is it on me?! It's on me!

> MIKE
> Dude, calm down. Just calm down. It's not on you.

Mike sounds brave but he is standing now too. Arms extended to his desk, arched over the computer with a visible concern.

> KAREN
> I'm going outside.

Karen walks to her door. It won't open. She pulls on it and rattles the knob, eventually kicking and slamming her shoulder against it.

> KAREN
> What the hell? What is happening?!

Everyone is moving to their exits. Shawn and Mike are off screen. Lizard cautiously approaches a window still in frame, darkened by curtains and a shade.

> LIZARD
> I am just going to...I have a feeling that...

He pulls down on the shape and it whips up. There is nothing there; no outside. Total darkness but solid, a black pit like a void of brick and mortar.

> LIZARD (cont'd)
> Oh my god. What the hell? What the hell is that?

Karen has come back to her computer and is watching the screen. She raises her phone to her ear; after a moment, lowers it, jams on the screen, and raises it again. This repeats while Lizard runs around screaming, banging on his walls and door.

Mike comes back on the screen, his phone also to his ear.

MIKE
Karen, are you getting anything?

KAREN
No, nothing. Won't even ring.

MIKE
Me either. I can't get out of my house. I can't get out of my own house!

He drops the phone.

Shawn comes back, carrying an axe and looking haggard.

SHAWN
I chopped my damn door down and there is a wall there.
There is a goddamn wall up to my house.

KAREN
It's not a wall. I don't know what is happening but this isn't real.

Lizard is starting to show signs of exhaustion.

MIKE
What's with this stupid color?

KAREN
It has to be connected.

MIKE
I hate it.

Shawn is cradling his forehead, the axe leaning on the wall.

SHAWN
Okay, we can't panic. We can't get out. We can't
make calls. What else can we do?

KAREN
Get a message online? I have been trying but nothing
else will load for me.

MIKE
Yeah, me either. No other page will open.

There is a pause, silence punctuated by frantic clicking. Lizard comes
back to the computer.

LIZARD
We are going to die.

Everyone responds at once. Mike cuts through.

MIKE
Liz, don't say things like that, man. We have to stay cool.

LIZARD
Man, we are screwed. Look at what is happening.

MIKE
We don't know what is happening.

LIZARD
Whatever it is, we are screwed.

SHAWN
Lizard, seriously man, stop.

LIZARD
You know I'm right. There is no getting out of this.

Karen's mic cuts as she raises her voice to a shaky shout.

KAREN
Stop it! What is wrong with you?! Stop!

Tears fill her eyes and Mike lets out a heavy sigh. Shawn picks up the axe.

MIKE
Yo, what are you doing?

SHAWN
Maybe we should smash our computers.

MIKE
Smash our computers? What the hell is that going to do?

SHAWN
I don't know. That's how it started, isn't it? Maybe it will stop it.

MIKE
Is it? Is that how it started?

KAREN
Yeah, where are you getting that?

SHAWN
I don't know, that's what happened, right? What happened?

LIZARD
Yeah, what was happening?

MIKE
Nothing. I was going to get a scotch.

LIZARD
Why are you always talking about your scotch?

MIKE
Really man, now?

KAREN
What were we talking about?

MIKE
I don't know, nothing. Bullshit.

LIZARD
Did you guys hear about that thing that fell into the ocean?

KAREN
Yeah, I saw the video. We watched the video! Didn't
we? Weren't we watching the video?

The question hangs.

SHAWN
I think so. There was a video. I remember that
big thing falling into the water.

KAREN
Were we watching it? Didn't we watch it together
just now? Is that what we were doing?

MIKE
I think…maybe it was.

SHAWN
So what's with this color?

Karen seems almost excited now.

KAREN
Oh my god guys, is this happening because we watched that video?

LIZARD
What, like some stupid creepypasta shit?

KAREN
Yeah! I don't know. I mean, but right?

Mike and Shawn are silent in thought.

MIKE
Maybe. I remember watching it. I don't know when else I could have
seen it. But, what happened? Weren't we doing something else?

KAREN
Yeah, you guys. I think something really weird is happening here.

LIZARD
So we are screwed.

KAREN
Let's just think. If this thing hit the ocean, and we watched the
video, and this color appeared, we got stuck in our houses…

SHAWN
Then nothing. That means absolutely nothing.

LIZARD
All of our connections are disabled too.

MIKE
Except for this one.

Another silence.

SHAWN
So it is this? This computer? Screw this then.

He rises, axe gripped.

MIKE
Woah woah woah, wait, man.

SHAWN
Why?

He is ready to chop.

MIKE
Just think. What if it doesn't work? This is all we have.

KAREN
Yeah, we at least have each other right now.

SHAWN
Is that helping?

MIKE
I don't know, but we should figure out before you fricking
chop your computer in half.

KAREN
For real, we need to try and figure out what is happening. Together.

SHAWN
Fine. But I'm about ready to chop through this wall.

LIZARD
Do you think that will help? It will just be the
same. It will stop you somehow.

The color continues to gradually grow

> SHAWN
> It? What is it?

> LIZARD
> I don't know, whatever is doing this.

> SHAWN
> Something is doing this?

> LIZARD
> Well, it has to be, right? What else?

> SHAWN
> It just happened.

> LIZARD
> Yeah, I guess.

Everyone looks puzzled.

> KAREN
> But the video. The thing in the ocean. It has to be related
> to that. It can't just be coincidence.

> MIKE
> Yeah, probably not. We don't know for sure but probably not.

> SHAWN
> So this thing falls into the ocean, we watch the
> video, and now we are all...trapped?

> LIZARD
> Makes more sense than anything else.

> SHAWN
> Does it?

> LIZARD
> Well, what do you got?

Nothing.

> KAREN
> Okay, so going with that...why this light? And
> why can we all talk but nothing else?

LIZARD
Maybe we are already dead and this is some kind of weird afterlife.

MIKE
That would be a huge letdown.

LIZARD
I don't know, maybe it disrupted space, time,
dimensions...some crap like that.

KAREN
And we're stuck in some kind of time loop?

LIZARD
Or something like that. Something we can't understand.
How would we know?

SHAWN
This is crazy.

LIZARD
I haven't heard anything better from you.

Everyone erupts, talking over each other again.

The light grows brighter. Its saturation increases with the rising tempers. Soon, each box on the screen is almost entirely painted over by the otherworldly hue, indistinguishable from one another.

Karen snaps out of it, stops yelling, and shuffles backwards.

KAREN
Listen, we need-

Everyone else is still talking over each other. They can't even see one another through the light and color. There is a high pitched ringing behind their voices.

The chat cuts. The screens go dark. Each of them are caught staring into an empty, black vortex, their own reflection hazily gazing back from the glass.

-

MIKE
Uh, hello?

He taps the power button on his laptop. Waiting for a response, he shakes the ice in his glass.

MIKE (cont'd)
Seriously?

The button is still unresponsive. He gets up and starts looking for the power cord. After a moment of rummaging he finds it and plugs the computer in. As he sits back down he presses the button but nothing happens.

He swigs his empty drink, letting the ice rattle against his teeth in frustration. Tension tightens the corner of his eyes into wrinkles. Abruptly, he realizes he is not alone.

Across the room, in the doorway, there is a figure. A shape at once both humanoid and alien. Its presence is unnatural. An anonymous shadow against the blinding color.

Mike jumps up, cries out, and stumbles backwards over his couch. He hits the floor with a thud.

MIKE
Who are you?!

Groggily, he pushes himself up and tries to straighten his vision. The shape is gone. The color is dimming. Everything seems to be coming into focus.

Then the walls melt. Pouring, like hot wax down themselves, they run as liquid into a mess. Behind them, a solid white barrier, not of any known material, seething with energy, is revealed.

Mike screams. His voice is fractured and echoed, cracking and repeating like a bad connection.

\-

> LIZARD
> Man, what the hell?

He jams on his keyboard ferociously. It's a childish attempt, a tantrum even he engages in without any confidence.

> LIZARD (cont'd)
> This sucks. We are so screwed.

Flopping backwards in resignation, he exhales theatrically. He runs his hand through his hair, tugging in frustration at the points it knots.

He doesn't notice the shadow figures emerging from the floor behind him. There are five, nondescript, completely indiscernible from each other. They loom over his back in complete silence.

The light in the apartment starts to fade. It takes him a minute to notice.

> LIZARD (cont'd)
> I knew it, I...

His grumble fades on itself.

Standing, he turns and finally faces the figures.

> LIZARD
> Woah, wai-

His mouth drops open and his eyes turn to olive colored saucers. Expressionless, he floats into the air, off his feet; levitating in a pained but absent posture.

The five forms shove long shadow appendages into his throat. They crackle and pop with white energy like lightning.

-

Shawn stares madly into his reflection on the screen. His eyes are wide and blood shot, the axe is slung over his shoulder.

The reflection doesn't look like him; doesn't move when he does. It seems to have a life of its own, acting independently as he tries to stay perfectly still, heaving chest and chattering teeth notwithstanding. Then it locks eyes on his. He feels paralyzed.

Somehow, it begins to morph out of the screen. It takes presence in the physical world, emerging from the glass screen like a body in the water.

The shadow is half out, mockingly arching over Shawn when his brain clicks. He screams and swings the axe, exploding the computer into pieces.

The being evaporates and the light begins to dim. Then, it surges and blasts through the house with a physical force. Shawn's ears ring, a high pitched siren in his head that brings him to his knees.

He drops the axe and covers his head, trying to muffle his mind. As the noise grows louder, he screams in harmony, losing grip of himself in the sound. The light pulses bright and sears his eyes, beginning to singe his skin and thin wisps of hair.

Shawn throws his body back, contorted in pain. He screams at the ceiling, cursing when he can. Blood leaks out of his nose and the corner of his eyes.

He hears chanting, a low alien hum, an unknown language of horrible consonants and consonance. It's worse than the light and the ringing, driving insanity into his soul; an emotion never felt before, something that couldn't come from the world.

His screaming stops but is still felt in the pink flame of the sound and color.

-

Alien lights drift through Karen's small room. Purple, green, red, blue, and back again.

Her computers are pushed aside, used up and useless. The door is still closed. It's an interior room - no windows - so the color seems to just materialize.

She listens, and waits, marveling at her own steady nerves. Something inside tells her not to look at her screens, not to cry, not even to move. She is perfectly still, prey from an invisible predator, trying to breathe as quietly as she can. Then she has to remind herself not to think about it too much.

A deep bellow shakes the room. Like hearing a whale song in its belly, reverberating like thunder trapped in the mountains, Karen relents an involuntary shudder. Her mouth cracks open to scream but she chokes it down.

She can feel something behind her. Not there, not yet, but probing from somewhere to make a connection. She can feel it, peering through static to get a picture, searching for her but unable to see.
Then the light begins to dim. The colors start to fade. The presence withdraws from the room, pulling away like a finished patrol.

Karen's room seems normal again. It is quiet and dark. There is no indication that anything happened.

She stays put. The computer screens spark back on but are dead, revealing dimly illuminated battery notices. She suddenly becomes aware of the ceiling fan spinning above her.

Karen takes a deep breath. Slowly, she stands. Her knees pop, of course, and she almost throws up.

Nothing happens. She eyes the door. It's still closed, but close. A rising heat sweeps her, like a flush of embarrassment.

She can't stay still any longer and bounds across the room. She rips the door open and races down the hall. Passing by a tiny, dirty kitchen, she slams into the front door and flings herself outside.

There are houses floating in the air. Everywhere, all around her, far off into the distance, homes and buildings levitate into the night, surging with white lightning energy, falling apart and revealing sterile alien structures underneath. The pods float higher and are stripped of their earthly parts, brick and wood and wire crashing to the ground below.

Karen can't think, doesn't believe what she is seeing. She smiles because she can and doesn't know what else to do.

KAREN
Good day to stay home.

YOU ONLY HEAR
THE MUSIC

Cindy Laughter left the bodega on a wet, sad night that seemed to invite memories in its street puddles and sidewalk swimming pools. The sky was as grey as the ground. There were less lights than usual; the canopy of the establishment had long gone dim and a severe lack of traffic was as palpable as nausea.

There was a poetry to the air. Everything felt melodramatic, like a scene from any New York movie ever. A black sedan pulled to the curb, singing in the rain. Cindy checked the license on her phone again before stepping in.
The driver was silent, didn't even say hello. That was fine with Cindy who tried not to drench his leather seats and awkwardly shuffled the paper bags in her arms that were about to burst.

She saw his yellow teeth in the rear view mirror and saw the blinding lights passing outside the window in murky, tear-shaped droplets down each block. The city stank and hummed; signs of life. Once she walked these streets, turning at the corners, on bright days with friendly faces. The fog that had covered everything stripped that away without an alarm bell; closing time came all at once.

Dead things lived in the fog. Ghosts, ghouls; whatever you wanted to call them. It descended like any other mist but brought with it insanity, and more tangible terrors. For a while the world tried to work, then it stopped. A new normal. The Death Wind; apparitions of an unknown origin that want to claw your eyes out.

The car pulled to the curb and Cindy hopped out. Heading into her building, she reminded herself to tip the driver generously for not bothering her. After a retinal scan, the barred door began to open like an automatic gate. A blue hologram of a 20th century mailbox blinked in the hall, reminding her of a message she already ignored.

Inside her room: however many feet by however many feet; a small place. Old world lamps with dolphins on the shade. A groovy light fixture in the center hung over a glass table lined in colored stones.

She pressed a button on the wall and a hologram of a woman appeared. Her features were different in obvious ways but otherwise she looked like Cindy. Her hair was long, where Cindy's was short, but they had the same sharp jawline. Cindy's eyes were brown but the hologram's were the same blue as the rest of her being. Cindy had dark hair but, blue again, the hologram's could be any color really; blonde - why not? - yet they had the same shape. They were like two people who liked the way the other looked but didn't want to admit it.

CINDY
Hi Carol. Anything new today?

CAROL
I have an incomplete message from Ramona
Fris. Would you like to hear it?

Cindy tried to suppress a shudder.

CINDY
No.

CAROL
Okay. There is nothing else new today.

CINDY
Thanks a lot, Carol.

CAROL
You are most welcome, Miss Cindy. Preference check:
do you still prefer me to call you Miss Cindy?

> CINDY
> Yes, that will do.

> CAROL
> Very well, Miss Cindy. Is there anything else I can do for you today?

> CINDY
> No, that will do.

> CAROL
> Very good, Miss Cindy. Please let me know if I
> can be of further assistance.

> CINDY
> Buzz off.

> CAROL
> Yes, Miss Cindy.

The hologram disappeared and Cindy returned to her motions. She went to a cupboard; white, with gold ordainment and a Victorian fashion - opening it to remove a parchment scroll and a glass canter of a decidedly alcoholic liquid.

> CINDY
> Carol, can you play Mozart?

The music entered low; soothing without disruption. Cindy sat by herself and poured a glass of the copper colored delicacy. She leaned back in her comfortable yet fashionable chair, listening to the gentle pelt of rain on the building.

By now, outside was surely a war zone. The fog was beginning to creep up to her windows, meaning a denizen of nightmares waited below. If Cindy opened her window she could probably hear the screams already.

She thought about how she had cut it too close. That's why her ride had cost so much, she was paying Fog Fare even though it hadn't hit yet. It was possible to go out in the fog. It was only fatal with prolonged exposure. So long as you were not in it long there could be almost no effect. Drivers and other service people who operated in the fog could command serious money. Because even a few minutes was enough to start the visions, inducing a disoriented state that only made it more likely to get lost and further enveloped in its endless madness. Once you marinated in it long enough, soaking and seeping, making you part of it, then the monsters would appear. They were real, bloodthirsty and ravenous. No one would be looking for you if you went missing.

There was no cause, no reason; no explanation for humanity yet. Society had adapted, largely fracturing into regional tribes. The internet persisted global culture but the threat made things like travel and international trade almost impossible.

Cindy missed the old world. She remembered it from her childhood but her functions as an adult only ever worked inside this paradigm. She had few friends; it was hard to get close. A federal job placement program had landed her as an accountant in a prestigious law firm, a seamless transition from education to employment that had allowed her to take a job in the inner city she had viewed as so dangerous when growing up in the surrounding suburbs.

The fog rose all the same, in city and town, busy street and empty countryside, unreliable but certain, like the weather. Here Cindy could at least reliably catch a ride to and from someplace close; she didn't have to drive a half hour just to get groceries.

Tonight she was planning on watching movies; old ones with actors like Seth Rogen and Steve Carrell. Films her mother loved that she had seen since she could remember; safe and familiar, happy bubbles of the past. It was the weekend and some wallowing was in order. Then there was a sharp knock at the door.

> CINDY
> Carol, who's here?

She stood as she spoke, anxiously sliding to the wall, edging towards the door.

> CAROL
> Projecting door camera.

23

A blue hologram, like Carol but fuzzier appeared in the living room. It was a tall, built man in a trench coat. His hat obscured his face from the angle of the camera.

                    CINDY
                  Who is he?

                    CAROL
          Identification not possible.

                    CINDY
              Crap Carol, really?

                    CAROL
I recommended that you install a second door camera, Miss Cindy.

                    CINDY
Buzz off, Carol. No, wait. Actually, I need you. Perform security
        check. Dim lights. Turn off music.

The house responded. Carol watched as the hologram of the man rapped again, the sound intruding through the space. She moved to the back wall and made her way to an adjacent bedroom.

It betrayed the elegant ease of the rest of the flat. Dirty clothes covered everything, books were stacked precariously on every surface, and a sloppily placed poster of Van Gogh's Starry Night accented one wall. Cindy rounded her messy bed, went to a little wood stand that had once been in her grandmother's house, and opened the wobbly drawer. She withdrew a small, sleek gun and exited back the way she came.

Another knock - the loudest yet. Cindy stood in the center of the room, pointing the gun through the hologram at the door. For the next knock, the man slammed his shoulder into the door and the hologram lunged forward, briefly startling Cindy.

He stepped back, making a runway, and charged. He threw his whole body into the door and broke through it entirely, sending splinters of wood and plaster flying through the air.

Cindy fired once but it missed, blowing a hole in the wall behind him. He straightened to face her and she tried to stop her hand from shaking the gun. His face was waxen and heavy, artificial like clay or heavy makeup. The eyes were lifeless, robotic, without the warmth of a soul. It looked human but was not.

Androids were not uncommon but never carried good news. They were the bouncers of society, or at least this model was. The ones serving more hospitable jobs were no longer designed to look like humans. The uncanny valley had prevailed and people never trusted them. Instead, those service droids took on more utilitarian appearances, like cute appliances. The Lifeless, as they were unceremoniously known, did the dirty jobs.

                    CINDY
          What the hell do you want?

                   LIFELESS
          Ramona sends her regards.

                    CINDY
    You can tell that psycho bitch I regret ever knowing her.

                   LIFELESS
    She wants to know if you enjoyed sleeping with Josh.

                    CINDY
          You have been following me?

She kept the gun trained on it. It dripped, wet from the rain, on her floor. They could take more damage than a human but a few well placed bullets would be enough.

                   LIFELESS
       Ramona says that she never loved you.

                    CINDY
       And you just came here to tell me that? Did
          you bring back my DVD player?

                   LIFELESS
          You are going to die.

It darted at her with inhuman agility. She fired three times, one bullet clipping its neck and another burying into its shoulder. It wasn't enough to stop it and it grabbed Cindy by the throat, lifting her into the air.

They froze like that, Cindy stuck in its grasp. She raised the gun but it grabbed her arm and twisted it all the way over, a crunchy snap and a scream from Cindy as the gun fell from her hand.

LIFELESS
I have been instructed to record a final message from you, for Ramona.

CINDY
Good, you can tell her Josh was ten times the lover that she ever was.

Cindy kicked, bucking the grip, striking the android's solid body and propelling herself backwards in a continuous motion. She hit the ground and rolled, cradling her broken arm close to her and grimacing with pain. She ran to the far wall, kicked open the window, and hopped out on to a fire escape.

Cindy recoiled back from the fog, which was heavy just below her feet, reaching up the rusted staircase and climbing over the sides. She peered back in, looking for the gun, but the machine was already pocketing it in its oversized coat.

If she went up she would be trapped. There was no choice.

CINDY
Bye, Carol.

CAROL
Goodbye, Miss Cindy.

The android was heading towards her and she started to scramble down the stairs. Below, the air was cooler and thinner. The temperature dropped as she made her way down, hurrying the best she could on the unstable structure.

Fortunately, she hadn't changed to her pajamas yet. Her sneaker hit the pavement with an able spring as she raced into the night. The fog blanketed everything, there was nothing to be seen; except a lone, dim blue light hanging in the mist, about 100 feet away. It was a Fog Terminal, a type of small structure that littered the city, little insulated pods where one could shelter from The Fog. That is all she would be able to do for now, as she had left her phone inside. Some of the Terminals had built in communication but she knew this one, outside her building, did not. She cursed herself for not calling a car as soon as she saw the man.

Still not being able to see anything through the fog, she was lucky to already know the way, and that it was free of obstacles. She hurried across the misty expanse, catching rays of the Fog Lights emanating from the building. Up close they could be blinding, but here, just a dash into the rolling clouds, they were filtered down to a haze that occasionally split to a streak.

She came to the Terminal and raised her hand to a sensor. Following the scan, an automatic door slid open on the fortified capsule.

Inside it was like a bus stop or a public restroom, dirty and run down in a way that only years of neglect could inflict. The air was fresh, thanks to the filtration system standard to each unit, but the floor was worn and the walls were aged to different colors. With another palm scan, a holographic map appeared that showed the surrounding area. The next terminal, which Cindy knew had a com system, was about two blocks away.

She could probably make it if she ran, she thought. Just a couple minutes in the fog could be hazardous but she knew the way. The bigger problem was the lifeless hunk of wires and machinery that would be following. She couldn't risk getting lost in flight; that would be the end of her.

She cursed Ramona, the crazy bitch. They had only seen each other for a year, and although the break-up hadn't been amicable, it didn't warrant hiring an android killing machine. At least, not in her mind. Ramona evidently felt differently.

Just then there came a pounding on the structure door. The sensor wasn't equipped to respond to androids, Cindy knew this, but it would only be a matter of time before it got in. It was weathered to sustain attacks from the fog, not from a cognizant, mechanical mercenary with a gun.

Instead of waiting, Cindy opened the door and shoulder checked the lifeless, springing from the pod like a pissed off butterfly from a cocoon. The man fell to the ground and its hat fell off, revealing handsome features that reminded her of Cary Grant. She stepped on its face as she vaulted over him and hit the ground running.

The fog was thick, like the dark beer that Ramona drank, Cindy thought. Then she realized that was stupid. Sorrow could come later. For now, she just needed to make it out of the city, out of the state - and out of the range of the android's likely perimeter restrictions. Among other things, jobs were paid on proximity, and if Cindy could just get far enough away, it would at least reset the clock when the lifeless had to update instructions.

Cindy ran blindly into nothing, pillows of white fluff clouding everything. She knew it would only be a few minutes before they started turning into monsters. She was definitely running the right way and didn't need to turn before the Fog Terminal; as long as she stayed on a straight course, it would be okay.

Then the stupid piece of shit tackled her, driving her down hard into the ground. She could feel the metal in its bony shoulder, the cold lifeless quality of its being. The ground poofed with the fog and she tasted blood in her mouth.

When she looked up she saw figures starting in the fog. Red eyes and sharp features, they materialized in the air from nothing. They were so close and the lifeless form on top of her pinned her down.

She elbowed the lifeless in the face, enough to create some space, and pushed herself to her feet. The fog monsters were ethereal but, she knew, still deadly real. She sprinted to the side to avoid them, losing her route in the process.

Then there was nothing: just blank, empty fog. Endless layers of wispy waves that she waded through, unsure of where she was going. Could androids see through the mist? She wasn't sure how that worked.

Every second longer increased the danger. She was about out of time. The fog wouldn't wait much longer. Soon she wouldn't be able to get away.

The terminal had to be close. She would have been coming up on it before, and although she had lost her sense of direction, it had to still be in front of her. She hadn't smacked into a building yet or made any purposeful change of direction. If it wasn't, it didn't matter if it was the monsters or the cyborg; there would be no surviving in such a dense fog.

Then she saw it, the hazy blue halo of light from the terminal. Her heart jumped into her throat. She could feel her pace quicken with hope. Always one to err on the side of caution, she had been trying to accept her death as inevitable the whole time. Suddenly, salvation was in sight. If she could get a ride, get far enough away, she might make it. There was no way Ramona had paid for a cross country hit job.

The terminal seemed like a chapel, an oasis, a place where dreams came true and anything could happen. There was nothing else around it, nothing in its frame; it was an island. At this point in the city, it should only take five, maybe ten minutes for a car to arrive - even in the heavy fog.

She scanned her palm and jumped back when the door opened, revealing someone inside. It was Ramona, the crazy bitch, her stupid ripped up denim jacket and dyed hair, that stupid smug look that Cindy had so grown to resent. Neither said anything.

Ramona raised a gun and shot Cindy in the face. Cindy fell backward into the fog, but it didn't matter now. It probably would have been better to die from the pesky fog monsters or that lifeless sack of shit than the person she had made love to two weeks before.

But she laid on the cold ground, with a blood splattered face, as Ramona stepped over her into a heavily armored taxi. The driver didn't care; who knows what happens in the fog?

THE SMOKY MOUNTAIN MONSTER

The Smoky Mountains, full of shadowed silence and un-touched grandeur, hum with stories and legends. There was a lit-tle log cabin in the woods that was said to have belonged to Davy Crockett. At night a deep mist would form over the leaf magenta grounds but no one was ever there to see it. A big rock rose like a monolith from a dirt patch where nothing else had grown for a long time.

No one ever saw it. A volcano could have splintered from the ground and moltend the forest while turning the sky to ash and it would be days before someone drove by an adjacent road and noticed. There was no one back here, the world had moved on and left this little stretch of existence to stagnate and freeze in time, with nothing to disrupt its trajectory. It slumbered.

So it sat for decades, time unfolding with callous change all through the world. Yet these few acres of country stayed oblivi-ous. Technology pushed, leaders grew and died, empires boomed and collapsed, but the few miles of trees around Limestone in southeast Tennessee rested in tranquility without any concern for what was happening beyond the borders. It felt at ease with its place in the world; a soft warm blanket for those who knew it.

This seemed destined to continue until suddenly it didn't. Some ambitious men decided to expand the real estate market further from the nearby market center. In less than a year, something that had been the same for lifetimes, secluded and undisturbed, was abruptly and violently uprooted, dug, plowed, shoveled, ripped, paved, molded, and shaped to be an entirely new area of the world fit for civilization and pleasant circumstances. The land did not agree and moaned its disapproval.

Families moved in fast and it wasn't long before the surrounding area was filled with gas stations and school buildings and soccer fields and fast food establishments. Year after year marched forward and before long the place the area had been for so long was forgotten, washed away in a tide of habitation. The development was a success but the earth did not reserve its protest.

The land grew haunted, wrecked by spirits and atrocities. Nothing else was allowed to inhabit this space. The very fiber of existence twisted in repulsion at its new form. There was something that revolted against what destiny was dictating. The new orchestra of everyday life - with all of its humanity and confinement - chafed against the fiber of all that had come before.

It was calm at first, residential troubles and local folklore. There was a haunted house or vengeful spirit. An entire barn of animals all perished overnight with no discernible cause. Some thought the lake was cursed. A family of five died in a fiery car crash on an unmarked road. A deranged man from a nearby slaughterhouse assaulted an elderly woman in her home. There was something damned in the space itself and it would endlessly produce whatever menace fit the void.

Generations disappeared down the family conveyor belt and the daily troubles of the place turned to twilight. Rumors of a ritualistic cult rooted in the community took hold. A flesh-eater preyed on the town. Some unknown beast, described in wild testimonies and interviews as a horned slug the size of a dog, turned the area into a tourist spot.

The 21st century had begun to wane when the fissure finally erupted. A great mass swelled in the land; bony, titanic shoulders lifted the earth into an illusion of mountains where there had been none. In the very spot where Davy Crockett's log cabin had sat the ground split and a tremor propelled through the surrounding countryside. A creature unlike anything ever rose to the sky, carrying the homes and barns and utility poles up to the clouds. All of that cursed land was swept up in an instant and crumbled to pieces on the back of the mile high gargantuan. It fell back to the land and crashed like haunted meteorites cratering in the surface.

The mammoth could not be. Its presence stained and contaminated the dimension of humanity. No reason or spirituality could support its nature. The thing was an intruder that trekked its cosmic mud across the carpet of conceived existence.

The impossible monstrosity evaporated to space in a fantastic fog. Time and gravity warped around it in a spectacular display of color that broadcast against the Smoky Mountain landscape. Geography twisted on itself in impossible spirals. Deep recesses swallowed rolling mounds. The seams of reality frayed and stretched as the entity joined the stars. The monster was never there, it couldn't be. Everyone already remembered the Tennessee canyons as all the land had ever been.

THE CAT LADY HOUSE

The Blogs Aren't for Reading Blog - July 5

Wow, I just had the craziest walk. In full disclosure I was high and drunk but I still think it qualifies as legit wtf. I purposefully waited for it to get dark because it's July and there is no way to describe how muggy and miserable the midwest summers can be in a way that hasn't been done a thousand times times before. It's true though and I did wait until dark because it was muggy and miserable.

It was okay enough when we, me and Pilkey of course, stepped out. (Sidebar for new readers, Pilkey is my dog. He's a stout, almost burgundy boxer, heavy like a tank - don't you call him fat.) I tied my hair in a ponytail to keep it off my neck but the sun had been down for a while so it was more that lingering hug of humidity than anything direct.

It was okay out but you don't care about that, you're not here to read about the in depth observations of my ordinary moonlit walk. So let's start there because it is something that recurred throughout: Google tells me it is a waxing crescent moon tonight and that sharp pointy fingernail sliver of a moon kept sauntering into my view at points, poking above trees and peering over rooftops.

I'm in a weird mood, I'll try getting to the point and then walking back through it. On my walk I stumbled on a crazy cat lady, a bunch of weird shit happened, and now there are a ton of cats outside my house. Seriously. Like it's still happening now as I write this and it's so weird and just whatever I don't know what to do but to start writing about it.

There's more to it than that because that doesn't sound so bad now that I write it but it was all really odd and creepy. Maybe eerie is the word? That is an underused word really and I think it better describes the hard to convey feeling I have right now. Like in

with the kid Damian and that dog and how it is just messed up.

Here's part of why everything that happened later with the cat lady was so unnerving: early on the walk I almost stepped on a dead cat, a roadkill cat to be precise, and I was already feeling jittery. Again, I was high and drunk so full disclosure is officially covered now.

I only made it a few houses down from mine when I had to start criss crossing the street to dodge trash cans. I have this thing about trash cans - I don't like being right next to them. Think about it - they are full of garbage and god knows what and all this gross and personal stuff a complete stranger never had to think about again and probably felt secure just tossing in the bin. Then all that shit gets drug down to the street and sits there, sometimes for god knows how long, cooking in the sun or marinating in the rain, drifting up into the air in a stench of microscopic particles and stinky vapors. It's gross af and I am not looking to bump up against anybody's disposables.

Unfortunately, when I deliberately planned my cool, fresh nighttime walk I neglected to consider that Wednesday night is trash night in my neighborhood. Since it was so late most of the receptacles already were parked on the sidewalk and I had to dart between them like Asteroids, while still being mindful of the traffic that tends to fly down the street at speeds that are clearly not advisable in a residential area.

Sorry, I am stalling. It's how I talk too but it's worse in writing because there is no one to stop me. Usually I can tell I am being extra by the glazed expressions of my comrades but in writing I just end up reflecting and talking to myself and making things even longer like this.

Anyways it was during one of these curbside pingpong sessions that I almost stepped directly on the corpse of curled up kitty. The body was by the side of the road - someone either hit it and at least moved it to the side so that it wasn't turned into raspberry jam on the burnt blacktop, or maybe it was just clipped anyway and gracefully landed in a resting place. It's the least that could be done, right? Or maybe something else happened, who knows.

Either way it so startled me that I was torn between trying to inspect the scene to make sure I was actually seeing what I thought I was seeing but not wanting to look much closer and see the grizzly details. Quickly it was settled by me having to drag Pilkey away from the scene lest he took too much of an interest (he hadn't noticed yet). God knows what kind of diseases or grossness can be transmitted from just a sniff of death.

I didn't really have time to process it because of this and my mind was racing already, then I spotted that weird moon over a ridge of trees in the nearest house's backyard. I felt a rush and like maybe I had watched too many horror movies recently. I turned the corner to the next street in a daze and all down that street I kept getting startled by ordinary people doing ordinary things. I just didn't really expect anyone anyway because it was dark and then I was so caught up in my head with what had just happened that someone standing off their back porch in the shadows with just the light of their phone on their face made me feel uneasy and when two guys suddenly broke from a house in conversation carrying a canoe (or some kind of skinny boat, I don't know give me a break) I literally jumped. For real, some guys with a boat made me jump in the air for no reason really.

I was recognizing that I felt overstimulated in a way I hadn't in a long time and I almost walked directly into a prone large tree that had been downed and left with a load of other shrubbery in a jungle trap on the sidewalk. Seems pretty irresponsible really but I should have been looking where I was going. I hope I didn't walk by any trash cans without thinking about it.

I really did almost walk right into it though, to the extent that I had to pull up on Pilkey's leash like the reins on a horse to stop him from walking into it too. I was wondering if I had really seen the cat or if it was just so dark and I was drunk enough that with my anxieties about the trash cans and the horror movies that I could somehow make that out of a splat on the ground, a shadow or smear of tar, the way some people see pets in the cloud or Jesus in their soup or whatever. Like a rorschach test.

At this point I was already thinking about writing this post and making sense of what I was going through. Then I came up on the church, stained glass windows lit with warm light from inside. In the parking lot a gaggle of teens, probably preteens judging by how much fun they were having and the giddiness in their laughs, circled the parking lot on those roller skates that have light-up color wheels. The kind that look like fireworks or ferris wheels, something that would have seemed amazingly futuristic to me as a kid. They are like the light up shoes from when I was young but sleek, on steroids, and rolling.

Seeing those bright, fluorescent, neon colors playing across the sacred parking lot made me think of Stranger Things. (Yeah, I watch way too much TV, but that's why you read this blog most of the time, right?) Something about the scene just felt really cool and retro, it gave me nostalgia and made me feel safe even in a weird world full of weird things. Oh, eerie, right? An eerie world full of eerie things.

This was also the next time I saw the moon. There it was again, wouldn't go away. Not even from the church.

The rest of the walk was uneventful, I tried to calm down and not read too much into everything. Even passing a partially constructed house and a torn down playground in front of a cemetery, I told myself not to get carried away. Mostly I was still obsessing over that cat and whether I had actually seen it, and if I should do something if I did. I started thinking I would call animal control if it was actually there when I went back by.

I'm dragging this out, I can't help it. I'm still high or drunk too I suppose, not really one distinctly but just a haze of intoxication that is fueling my adrenaline and weird "what the hell just happened to me?" vibes. Sorry this is really long and about nothing.

When I went back down the street and was almost home I started looking real closely for the dead cat. I was so disoriented earlier that I couldn't remember exactly where I thought I had seen it so I was watching every shadow and patch of darkness real closely because I was afraid I was going to step on it still. Then there was some traffic - cars going too fast down the road again - and I had to dodge trash cans. Someone stepped out of a house with their phone in their face and I thought I would just forget the whole thing and walk home. Head hell high, stop looking at shadows, and forget about it. Resignation!

Well, as soon as I thought that some poetic justice hit and I saw the poor squashed kitty by the road. There it was, it had happened, it wasn't imagination or drunken tripping or whatever. Poor kitty.

I hardly had time to process this when I noticed two women standing in the yard of the most run down house on the street. And bam it happened real fast, there were suddenly cats everywhere. Like seriously so many cats, it was stupid. There must have been a dozen or more just on the porch behind the women, eyes glowing yellow and all that regular creepy cat stuff. Most of them sat attentively, gaze already on me, like overbred tail-flicking statues.

Man there were so many cats it was instantly what the hell. More off along the side of the house, disappearing out back to the woods. I realized immediately that these stupid people keep too many cats and obvioulsy can't keep them safe or care for them since there was one dead in the road right outside their house.

The women seemed like ordinary ladies, an old lady and her middle-aged daughter probably. They were clearly feeling caught in conversation as they eyed me silently. The grandma lady was in a house robe that she held tightly to her, clinging on the fabric. The other woman was a total Karen in jean shorts and everything. I could feel them just staring at me as I tried to drag Pilkey by the sentinel army of staring kitty cats.

It turns out the people were actually pretty nice. While I awkwardly tried to shuffle by in complete silence, eyes probably glossy from booze and grass (who says grass anymore? I really do feel like writing), the older woman finally offered a hello. I waved and she asked me how I was doing, I think I said something about the weather. The other lady didn't say anything but the old woman was actually nice, almost apologetic like I caught them in something but they knew I didn't know what it was. She smiled and the jean shorts lady didn't really look at me. Eventually she clapped at a cat that was getting too close to the road, scaring it back to safety.

I kept walking for a minute while wondering if I should say something about the roadkill cat. Did they know already? Is that why they were being weird? Or would me telling them set off some torrential outpour of grief and shock? I didn't want to do that to the old woman especially and how was I going to handle all of this with Pilkey and the army of felines?

As I was considering this I suddenly heard some kind of weird laughter from the woods. I can only describe it as a cackle, it was uneven and primitive but distinctly human. Nothing else on earth that I know of could have made that kind of sound. It wasn't right, I felt the natural instinct to flee. It was menacing and indifferent all at once; callous and prowling.

It was so unsettling that I turned to look if the women heard it. I don't know why really, I had not trusted them seconds before but now they felt like a lifeboat at sea. They were at least there and human and must have heard what I did too.

But they weren't there. I was alone on the street and never saw or heard them go. They just disappeared, did they run from the sound? The old woman couldn't have moved that fast. I don't know what happened. But all of a sudden it was just me staring at a porch full of cat eyes that didn't seem to mind the strange noise from the woods.

I was figuring out that it must have come from behind the house, or somewhere in those surrounding woods but definitely in that direction, when it laughed again and this time even closer.

It wasn't really a laugh but it sounded so happy in a disgusting, mean way.

The cats still seemed unphased which I thought was weird since it had such a predatory sound. I booked off and ran straight home, literally pulling my poor dog along the way (sorry, Pilkey). I was back in the house and locking the door before I thought about anything else.

It was all scary and weird and I still don't know what to think of it but I probably could have gone to bed and forgot. The laugh could have been some kid or a weirdo or some weirdo kid or whatever. The sound was inhuman, unlike a noise I can imagine any person making. Maybe that's my imagination (or the grass) and it could have been anything. The way the women disappeared scared me so much, they were right there and then just gone. Seemed impossible. And the creepy cats staring at me like nothing mattered. It was all creepier than it sounds but I was high and drunk and it could have been anything.

Since I have been home there have suddenly been a lot of cats outside. It's like they followed me home and they are all around the house. I guess I should call animal control but it's night, so maybe I should call the cops. Can you call the cops on cats? It's just so eerie and there are tons of them, they have been up in my windows and staring through the screens. I could be imagining it but I thought I have heard that cackle too, the same laugh somewhere out there. I'm going to sound crazy if I call someone, like there's a bunch of cats and someone laughing at me, so I am writing this instead. I have been dragging on here because I don't know what to do and had hoped this would help me make sense of it. Instead I am filled with more of a foreboding than before, realizing I think that all of this really doesn't seem right, and they are still outside. I can see one of them now trying to peer through the curtain and I hear that crazy laugh closer than it was in the woods. I guess I am going to post this and try to call someone. I'll probably be embarrassed about it tomorrow and wondering why I thought cats were laughing at me. The noises are at the door now so this is it.

THE TOOTH FAIRY

Edward had a hole in his tooth. It hurt when he ate, drilling through the meat of his face, singing chords of pain in his skull. He had tried to take care of his teeth but failed.

When he was little, his dad told him to brush regularly but he never did it after every meal. He had work done at the dentist since he could remember. The way his father spoke so reverently of mouth hygiene, he sensed a deep trauma there all along. When his own dental state deteriorated, it felt like a bit of destiny.

Maybe he should have flossed more. He tried to brush in semi-circles for two whole minutes, as instructed, but he never flossed. He didn't like the way it felt, this junky stretch of wire sliding through saliva and raking against enamel. Maybe that would have saved all the pain.

Food would get lodged in the cavernous hole, stick there and poke at his gums with little daggers for hours after eating. The feeling was infectious, invasive, with a hurtful rhythm that pulsed, and subsided, only to grow back. His drinking swelled, flooded his lungs. He poured straight liquor on his sore mouth. He should have gone to the dentist but didn't.

When he first heard the voices he thought they were in his head. Then he thought they were in his walls. Finally, after weeks of sloshing cheap whiskey, vodka, gin, tequila, and rum in his mouth, he heard the voice in his tooth.

It was tiny but able, confident though indecipherable. The whispers rose all day long, languishing in waves like the tide coming in. He heard them more and more until a hum of nonsense cast him deaf.

Then he reached into his mouth, one morning when the coffee was stale and a piece of bacon from his egg biscuit sliced off and cut into his wound, and gripped that corpse of a molar. It was loose and wiggled like ripe fruit for that famous fairy; the one with coins for body pieces. The tooth creaked and squirmed in the bloody pink tissue.

He ripped it out and gore flew through the air in fountains. It poured over the house, caking the walls and the ceiling in fluids and human debris, enough for a congregation of people. The cacophony of innards flooded the room, washing up to the windows in an angry churn like the sea. Bones hit the wall and pierced through plaster.

Edward's face split open and erupted in a collage of fungi. Vines shot from his teeth and weaved into the house, gripping framework and entangling with wiring, fusing to the pipes and structural shell of his home.

Outside the ground rot. Holes opened in the soil, plunging forever deep in cavernous vacuums. Slick pink membranes formed like slopes in the land.

Edward, no longer Edward but an evolving mass of mushrooms and roots and flowers, churning vines and jagged branches, grew through the roof. The famous last words of the house as it groaned from the strain before exploding in a burst like vomit. His last thought, the tooth ripping from his jaw.

It stinged and poisoned the environment, spreading through the surroundings like a fever. Everything withered and decayed to its touch, transformed and conformed to its nature. The entire surrounding area, a neighborhood bordered by trees, erupted into its tune. The reach grew, to a nearby shopping center where the buildings crumbled and the earth swallowed parking lots.

A mold crystallized on the mushrooms first, then tiptoed to the branches, traced the vines, strangled the flowers. It covered the earth, racing behind the consumption of forest-things. No being existed in it anymore, it spread uninhibited across all things. The world was remade in its image and then shrank and forgot.

OUR HOUSE

In the middle of the second winter in their new home, he saw the wretched hag monster holding their baby in a split second flash that fractured his mind. Tracy and Adam Brinkett had bought the house in the spring of the prior year. She had taken his name the summer before, around the same time that they upgraded to being a family. Blake, a curly haired baby boy, joined them in the strangely shaped, pastel blue house almost as soon as the papers were signed.

One of the things Mr. Brinkett had liked best about the house was a pair of bedrooms in parallel at the end of a Y-shaped hall. The hall ended in a strange indentation, a kind of point in the wall, and the rooms were across one another; respectively on each side of the divider. It was an unusual arrangement but Adam had thought from the beginning it would be nice to have the baby's room so close and imagined how he could peer around the corner from their room and see straight into the nursery.

The first year passed rather uneventfully, as Blake slept in the bedroom with them. A few times Adam heard bumps in the night and Tracy once thought she saw something moving in the walls, bulging and slithering like a snake in the plaster, but neither could ever find evidence or confirm their fears. Tracy had been drinking that night and it was the first time she smoked pot since the baby.

After the first birthday, Blake moved into the adjacent room so that the tired but happy couple could actually start sleeping on a regular basis. Immediately, Adam heard crying in the night but whenever he checked on the baby there was nothing. He figured that it was just the matter of being in a new place.

But then strange apparitions became a common occurrence for the family. Adam awoke violently in the night after seeing something in the room and Tracy told friends she would see a shadow in the corner that vanished when she turned. They even talked about speaking to a priest or enlisting the help of a paranormal investigator but the few times Adam looked online the search results did not inspire confidence.

The happenings escalated in severity and frequency. The stove top would light full flame for no reason and the thermostat would drop to freezing temperatures. The blankets would be pulled off Tracy as she slept and Adam found himself waking from sleep while walking around the house. Once, with friends over, all of the power in the house went out and the next morning no one could remember the time that had passed or how they got home.

The Brinketts put the house for sale the next day.

The night before they were set to move out Adam detected a strong smell of sulfur through the house. He thought about leaving, taking Tracy and Blake to a hotel by the airport where they were set to depart from to their new home in Cleveland the next day. Adam had been able to easily relocate within his company and Tracy felt optimistic about a change in scenery and returning home after years in sunny New Mexico. But Adam was ready to go to bed and figured he would only sleep a few hours anyway for the 6am flight. Maybe he would even get up a little early.

He went to sleep that night with a streaming playlist serenading the background. They were eager to leave but even with all the uneasiness he couldn't help reflect romantically on the days they bought the house and welcomed Blake into their life story. That first Christmas; when it was still easy enough to believe that this would be the home they shared the rest of their lives. That now seemed like a distant memory as their bags waited on the couch and most of their belongings had already been shipped to the new place back in Cleveland with Tracy's family.

While dreaming of a park bench submerged on the ocean floor, Adam awoke to the sound of wailing. He was just struggling to consciousness but the cries seemed more fervent than usual. Tracy had told him they should move the crib to their room but Adam had insisted that with the narrow divide between the rooms it was all the same. The truth was that he had just wanted to make love that night and when it next occurred to him the flight had already been booked. The house had been quiet for a while and the family even slept peacefully for consecutive nights.

The flesh of his bare feet slapped against the hardwood floors. Pockets of color took shape in the shadows as his eyes tried to adjust to the changing light in the hallway. He craned around the corner, bridging that Y-shaped hall, bracing against the strange indented point in the wall to peer into the nursery like he did every night before bed.

His heart sagged and his mind erupted when in the other room he saw a fat, wrinkled, ghoulish woman with long strands of tangled black hair staring back at him, standing above the crib with Blake cradled in her arms. She held him tenderly, supporting his head with a careful touch, as thick liquid slimed off of her and soiled the floor. Her dark eyes were like torches of marble and as she gazed back at Adam she hissed, a roar that shook the house and sent a primal, suffocating sense of panic through his core. Madness swirled in his head and a terrible sound echoed through him that he could feel in his fingertips.

Instinctively, Adam heard himself scream "This is our house!"

But it wasn't. The bags were already packed and she held their baby.

FIREWORKS

"What was that?" Ezra yanked his head sideways. His headset shuffled through the microphone. Outside his window, a loud boom echoed through the streets.

"Okay, I guess I have to go. I'll sign back on later." The young boy shut down his computer. He had wavy hair that flirted with his shoulders, parting in the middle. He wore a hoodie for an obscure indie game and pajama bottoms, which had been cropped out of his stream.

This was the third such reverberation in the last half hour. They cracked like a gunshot and shook the house. Ezra was surprised it hadn't woken his parents. It was after midnight and his father was known in the neighborhood for having shouted rants in his evening gown before.

The first two shots Ezra dismissed, live on his stream, as "probably a car backfiring" (with "do cars still do that?"as the punchline). He absent-mindedly wondered if it could be his neighbor, Mr. Armstrong, shooting off fireworks. Although two weekends after Labor Day it was closer to Halloween than the Fourth of July, Mr. Armstrong had long been recognized as a connoisseur of things that go boom.

Still, by the third explosion in the cool September air, Ezra thought something seemed weird. He crept through his parents house, peeking through the windows along the way to the adjoining yard of Mr. Armstrong. All was dark.

Another shock wave rippled the night as Ezra crossed through the family living room. A brand new TV hung on the wall and pristine coffee table books glistened on a glass table in the center of the room. Pictures of Ezra with his parents were framed and perched on the entertainment center, a book shelf, and the decorative ridges on the archway to the kitchen.

The next boom rattled those picture frames. A bright light flashed across the room, capturing Ezra as a shadow on the wall. It illuminated the whole house, first in a dazzling white and then pulsing through the rainbow.

Ezra thought about just going back to his game. After all, if it was Mr. Armstrong, what was he going to do about it? It might be against city ordinances or whatever but it's not like he was going to call the police. Although Mr. Armstrong loved fireworks, and annually put on a show that rivaled the city's official celebration, it wasn't like him to cause such a ruckus so late at night. He sometimes had blown off excess supplies late into the fall, but never at such a delicate hour. If Ezra were to find him launching missiles in the backyard, would he do anything about it?

Nonetheless, he opened the front door and stepped outside. As he did, the distance roared again. Now that he was out of the house it sounded further away. Still close, but not next door.

Ezra took a minute to adjust to the cool night. In September the air nips and teases, it's refreshing and drinkable.

He stepped down the stairs, slipping off the porch onto the walkway colored by solar lights staked in the ground. Across the street they had already decorated for Halloween. The small yard was aglow with orange lights and pumpkins. An oversized inflatable Grim Reaper towered nearly to the gutters of the house.

Ezra found himself in the street, walking down the middle white line, perpetually being swallowed by the darkness. There were houses to the side but the shadows hung so heavy as to lock them away.

The light from the next boom spelled colors of impossible shades across everything. It was dazzling in the sky, bright and pure, just for a moment. Then the inky night welcomed him back.

He suddenly saw something coming down the middle of the street towards him. The line of existence that seemed to tether them together - that pulsing shaky white strand in the road - vibrated and danced. The Thing was massive but frail; gargantuan yet thin - impossible.

He tried to back away but like a projection it grew before him, the ground beneath his feet transforming to treadmill, pulling endlessly and bringing the shape closer.

Ezra opened his mouth to scream but a black hole expanded across his face. All the darkness around him warped in tangible evanescence. The creature was upon him.

It was hideous and alluring, impossible to perceive. The skin was white like old meat, it stood more than seven feet tall. Its face was shadowed and maddening; just the shape was indecipherable. With long scythe-like arms it impaled him with everything he ever had been and wanted to be.

***

BOOM!

The force of the noise shot Shirley up in her bed. Above her, plastic glow in the dark stars orbited on the ceiling. They were beginning to fade from years of shining but still lit the room in a gentle warmth.

The sound seemed to hang in the air and reverberate in the walls. Picture frames that sprouted in clusters on the top of a solid oak dresser shook; one fell to the floor and shattered. Shirley was on her feet, alert and attentive, with a spryness that surprised her.

She was 18, barely over 5'5; fit, thin, dressed in a tank top and gym shorts. Her dark hair was pulled back in a long ponytail and she had fallen asleep without removing her makeup. The windows on the opposite side of the room gaped like a vortex to the cold night that pressed against them.

Another audible shockwave rattled the door. Before she thought any more about it she pulled that door open and ran from the room. It felt like a tunnel caving in or a building being bombed. Somehow, whatever it was felt like it was getting in.

Shirley bounded down the stairs, nearly slamming into the wall, skipping the last few steps in a stumble. Her father had already gone into work for the night, the house was empty. Empty, save for her and whatever was trying to get in.

She raced to the front door and threw her body against it, checking the lock and the bolt. Peering outside, she was careful to keep herself low. There was nothing in the street, only her car; a beat up, sagging hunk, parked with two wheels on the curb. She tried to hear something beyond the crickets but the neighborhood seemed silent.

Then there was a great flash, the road and houses briefly clear as a summer day, and a terrible blast of noise. It was the same boom from before but sounded almost more like a horn now, shaking Shirley and throwing her gut into her mouth. She opened the door; she didn't know why, she didn't think about it. Somehow, it felt like it would abate the pressure growing in her head from the blasts.

The crisp, moon soaked air rushed around her legs and up

through her home. Outside suddenly seemed alive and dangerous, full of possibility. The street held a palpable appetite.

Shirley stepped on to the porch, a well-maintained facade of home-liness. No one had sat out there, on those wicker chairs, with the song of the wind chimes and smell of the bushes, for many years. Not since her mother was alive.

The yard passed around her in a blur, she was out in the street while she still thought about the last time she sat out there with her dad; a spring day more than five years ago, after the funeral. They had not really spent any time together since then, just passing meals around the dim kitchen or obligatory check-ins after school in the living room.

The road wanted to keep stretching out forever. Her surroundings fell away and even the moon seemed to vanish. She felt hypnotized by the pattern she followed.

A new boom split colors in the air where there had been none. It seemed to fracture the picture of reality in shapes like cracked glass. Every house around her was suddenly red, aghast and gargantuan, filled with shadows.

There was something in the road. It moved down the middle to-ward her. She saw teeth - fangs - and long, impossible arms. It felt like a bowling ball sinking through her digestive system.

The thing rushed at her. Not like an animal, or anything in the natural world, but with a halted, skittish advance; like a video skipping frames. She screamed, she tried too, but she felt her mouth expand across her face. As the creature reached her, she felt a suction in dimensions that lurched her organs inside her. The beast ran its talons through her and she disappeared.

***

Ezra's eyes blinked open. A fog covered void stretched endlessly around him. Thick, billowy puffs of cloud rolled along the black floor and turned to mist across the expansive darkness in every direction.

He pushed himself to his feet and rubbed his head, massaging the pain. A sound still echoed in his ears, the last firework he heard hanging like a ghost in his head. Lights and colors pulsed in his eyes.

Stumbling through the knee deep fog, he spotted a silhouette prone on the ground before him. It was a girl, pretty and face down in the mist. She had a ponytail and wore heavy makeup.

Ezra fell into the fog to lift her.

"Hey, are you okay?"

He turned her over, onto her back, and elevated her head with his hand. It felt strangely intimate but the fog would cover her face otherwise. She was probably only a year or two older than him.

She stirred awake. Her eyes blinked open. She regarded him sleepily at first; then, a pure terror filled her face.

Shirley pounced to her feet and pushed Ezra back. He floundered, falling backward and sinking into the fog. She ran in the opposite direction, feet pounding into the vague night.

Without warning, fireworks filled the air. Huge explosions of dazzling beauty ignited the empty space and filled the dark with color. They were all around her, above her head, so loud they forced her to her knees, into the fog.

Ezra, up from below, grabbed her by the shoulders. Helping her to her feet, the two ran the few paces back to where they were. The show stopped; the fireworks faded.

"What the hell?!" Shirley shaked as she screamed, stepping forward into Ezra's face.

"Woah, chill! I don't know. I don't know!" Ezra rattled around too.

"What do you mean? Where are we? Who you are?" Shirley shoved Ezra. He almost fell over again.

"I told you, I don't know! I woke up right before you. We were just...here." He trails off at the end, his eyes reflecting reminiscence.

Shirley stopped, seeming to consider something on her own. Her eyes filled with fear again as something dawned, the memory of what happened before. She locked eyes with Ezra.

"What is the last thing you remember?"

"When? Now? You pushing me around."

"No, not now. Earlier."

"Earlier like when this happened?'

"Like before."

Ezra paused, running through it in his mind.

"It's kind of blurry. But there was this noise, a boom. I thought my neighbor was shooting fireworks. Then there was this...thing. In the road."

He barely finished the last few words. His eyes returned Shirley's stare.

"What about you?"

She thought for a moment in silence.

"I also saw something in the road. And heard a noise."

The two scanned each other, then looked around at their sur-roundings. It was beginning to dawn that neither could help the other. The fog seemed even higher, now almost up to their waist.

"So what do we do?" Shirley's voice was friendlier than it had been.

"Get out of here?" Ezra looked around aimlessly.

Then something appeared in the fog in front of them. It was the beast, pale and gargantuan. Somehow the thing was clearer in the flood-ing fog. Taller than any man, it towered on long muscular legs that seemed oversized for its thin, anemic frame. The arms were varyingly long, reaching out and rippling back like a stretch toy.

For the first time they saw its face - really saw it. The visage was more than hellish, more than a monster. It was sawed in half, straight down the middle so the skull was split and the innards exposed, a dark grey skeletal structure, and jagged teeth erupted in the colorless mem-brane.

Ezra and Shirley were running already, blindly into the fog. There was nowhere to go but it didn't matter. They must be anywhere but here.

The fireworks started. Fake flowers in the area without sky. They increased in occurrence and severity as the pair made it further.

The thing was behind them. It was getting closer, seeming to draw them towards it in the blank space like an escalator. Light itself seemed to dissipate and flee from the black mask that vortexed its face.

The booming noise, the feeling of pursuit; Ezra and Shirley both screamed, unheard by each other or even themselves; screamed and ran aimlessly. There was nothing but fear and misery, a feeling of gripping, sinking dread, extended endlessly by the animalistic instincts of pursuit. It was all consuming, all knowing, until it felt like it was all that there ever was.

***

BOOM!

Vance Inescort walked down the middle of the road. His skin gleamed in the streetlights. He was of average size, short hair, handsome features. He wore black shirt and pants, with the silver chain of a pocket watch reaching across his hip.

Brilliant shades of every color flowed through the sky. The fire-works were constant, an uninterrupted barrage - some soundless and hurried in the procession. Vance walked, hypnotized, as fog formed along the edges of the road.

A great shape formed in the distance in front of him. It seemed too small to be visible at first, the scale defying all sense of reality as it grew in approach. The horrible sight, a creature not crafted by nature, drew upon him.

Vance steeled himself. His spine locked into gear and his head cocked to the side in curiosity. He didn't seem bothered by the impending monstrosity.

As the thing crept nearer its horrible stench filled the air. There was a slopping and sliming sound, like a stinky mop sloshing around. It was muscular; towering like a bodybuilder, about to rip through its shell.

Vance Inescort looked into its shadowed face with bemusement.

"Well, what are you? Haven't seen anything like this before."

Suddenly, Vance exploded into a possessed torrent. Fangs flashed in the night and his features twisted into a furious grimace. His long fingers seemed to stretch and expand, forming into razor talons that slashed through the air.

Vance was on the thing, biting and clawing as it reeled in shock. Long slices of the pale flesh skewered through the air like sautéed onions. Blood splashed against his face and drenched his clothes.

His fangs sunk deep into the beast. He pulsed and squirmed with power, sucking the entity from itself. A million fireworks went boom in his head.

***

Shirley and Ezra awoke in a long grass field; a football field, situated outside of a small, Lego block high school. Shirley tried to hurry to her feet but floundered on spaghetti legs. Ezra felt like he couldn't move, like a spider trapped on one of those death mats.

"Now how the hell did we end up here? What the fuck?" Shirley looked over to an again marquee sign that displayed dates of football games and other school activities, crowned with a Mt. Carmel High sign.

Ezra was still on the ground. He couldn't even talk, the muscles in his face feeling as cemented as the rest of his body. He made a vain noise in his throat and shifted his eyes around.

Shirley knelt and was about to say something when she spotted something moving across the field toward them. It was still foggy, though not in an otherworldly fashion as it had been in that dream-like hell. Now it was just normal foggy. The silhouette gained yards down the field unimpeded, the absence of defensive linemen allowing the ground to be taken effortlessly.

Ezra still couldn't move as Shirley started to scream. They could tell already this shape was not to be trusted. It advanced on them with a deliberate aggression, an unmistakably malignant purpose. Something in its stride seemed to betray its intent.

As the being emerged from the shadows into the overhead slights of the scoreboard, its form became more clear in the mist. It had the body of a person; strong arms, and a ripped torso caked in dried blood. But its neck splintered and flowered out into a hideous stump with tendrils lined in razor fangs twisting in the air. It was in a sense decapitated but had fleshy roots reaching for the sky.

Shirley somehow forced Ezra to his feet. Deadweight, he finally got his legs and gathered himself upright, the cold air like petroleum in his breath. The two shambled away, so afraid and desperate that direction didn't matter.

They wandered aimlessly into the dark, away from the field and towards the school. Mt. Carmel High was an unassuming brick building, a rectangle with an expansion wing that connected to make a rotated L. Its diminutive stature was accented by the eternal range of mountains that loomed in the distance.

Ezra was able to walk on his own by the time they reached the front door. It was locked but Shirley was undeterred. She immediately led them back down the stairs and off the pavement, around the side of the building. At the junction of the expansion they came to a small gap in the structure that housed a fire exit. There were also two windows on the opposite wall - high enough to not be reached.

"That second window is unlocked, I used to break in here with my friends all the time." Shirley walked to the end of the structural enclave and pulled a step stool from the grass.

"You broke into the school? Why? When?" Ezra was sincerely incredulous.

"At night, on the weekends usually. We smoked, ya know. Hung out." She placed the stool beneath the window as she spoke.

Ezra watched her, wanting to help but unsure of what to do. The adrenaline was wearing off and for the first time since waking from that foggy state in the football field, he felt the real sharp twist of fear. He could barely remember anything. Horrible flashes were coming to him all at once as he saw Shirley step on to the platform and prop the window open. Instantly she was gone, sliding gracefully through the window and into the building.

He suddenly felt very alone and could hear the crickets deep in the night. The air felt still and he waited for that nightmarish nothing monster to spring from the corner. Finally it dawned on him that he should follow; he didn't know why he was waiting.

He clambered up on to the little stool and, with a strained groan, forced himself clumsily through the window. His entrance lacked all of the poise that Shirley had displayed. He stumbled forward and fell head first, down to the other side.

As soon as he landed there was a deafening BOOM, like it was directly outside the window. It sounded so close that Ezra felt like it was following him inside. Bright colored light flashed and illuminated the interior.

It was a restroom and it could have been any restroom in any school anywhere ever. The tile was old and worn but not dirty. The stalls, paper towel dispensers, and mirrors above the faucets were ordinary. A nondescript and indifferent refuge.

Ezra set himself upright, untwisted a crooked neck, and rubbed the bump on his head. Shirley was not there. He struggled to his feet and drug himself to the door.

The hallway was obscured in the haze of night. Shirley was already down at the other end, peering through a pair of green doors. "Hey, what's going on? What are we even doing here?"

Shirley didn't answer. She cracked the door open and put one foot inside. Ezra watched, her one leg anchored in the hallway, the rest of her leaning into complete darkness.

"Yo, what are we doing here?" He kind of whispered but sounded too anxious to control his volume. He started toward her.

His steps echoed down the hall. Die-cut humanoids were strung together, hand in hand, along the wall. A row of lockers formed on the left side and Ezra's shadow stalked across them as he proceeded.

Shirley suddenly reappeared from the doorway. "You have to see this," was all she said before stepping into the black beyond the doors.

***

Shirley entered the gymnasium. When she came here with her

friends - Barry, Les, and sometimes Eve - the gym would be dark; only the peripheral glow of an exit sign, the dark silhouettes of the basketball hoops, and the bleachers in the gloom. Now though there were fireworks - inside the gymnasium, perfectly contained; controlled to explode in harmless fire showers below the ceiling.

She walked toward them, not quite a trance because she knew the impossibility of it and worse what it implied; she felt the fear running through her. There was nowhere else to go. She had to look.

Vaguely she registered Ezra entering behind her. She heard the door swing and slam shut. Then his scream; he was calling to her. He called her name.

BOOM!

There was a dazzling flash, the blast seemed closer than the others. It interrupted their rhythm at its own interval. They continued, like a chant, as the hideous nothing, the tumor like monster appeared in the air.

"Shirley!"

She finally heard it clearly.

BOOM!

The thing screeched and rushed toward her. She turned and ran. Ezra held the door open and when she nearly tripped by, he slammed it shut.

The abomination burst right through them, blowing both doors clear off their hinges. It roared furiously as the lights from the fireworks spilled out of the gym and barely made it onto the scene in strange shadowed shapes.

"Come on, this way!" Shirley had regained herself.

She was scared that she had almost succumbed to its game. If Ezra hadn't been there, she felt like she would have walked right to it. Already, as she led him back down the hall, she reasoned that it was only fair for having carried him across the football field earlier.

"This way, I know a place." She took his hand, not out of affection, but because he was beginning to fall behind.

"Yeah, that worked out so well last time," Ezra replied snarkily.

They went down a flight of stairs, the small school at least being afforded a lower level with a few extra classrooms. Shirley pulled them toward a door at the end of the hall.

Inside was a music study. Rows of chairs waited, forever if necessary, for someone to take a seat. Music notation painted the whiteboard and a piano sat at the front of the class, ordinary but authoritative.

The two shuffled through the room like tardy students. Without a word, Shirley slid open a panel of wall to reveal a spacious storage compartment. She went right in but Ezra hesitated, incredulous.

"What's the plan?" He tried to ask calmly but could hear the impatience in his own voice.

"We're hiding. What's your plan?" She also sounded annoyed, waiting to seal herself away with the wall.

"I don't know but...won't we be trapped? If it finds us?"

"Hasn't it somehow just shown up everywhere this whole time? I would rather hide than find myself walking to it again."

Ezra conceded. He had no other suggestion. He slid into the space beside her and she shut the compartment from the inside.

***

There was no BOOM when the thing crept into the room. The door inexplicably flew open but then it was silent. The creature entered, its muscular arms glistening still and its sacrilegious neck appendages swirling and twisting on themselves.

Ezra and Shirley waited in the wall. They trembled and tried not to breathe heavily. Although they couldn't see the beast they knew it was there; the presence was unmistakable.

Shirley suddenly felt like this wasn't going to work. She was so sure of herself a moment ago, leading them here, but it was all fear and instinct. Now she realized they were trapped; backs against the wall. And she had led them here.

Ezra was already trying not to hyperventilate so she tried not to betray her revelation. Silently she scanned the compartment they were in for a clue, anything that could help. There were only instruments, a large, scuffed-up tuba, a skeletal drum set, some things she didn't recognize, and a violin, with its bow.

The monstrosity, seemingly picking up on a scent, started launching the chairs into the air. The room was quickly being cleared out, with it drawing nearer to them in its furious path. Shirley knew it would find them.

She grabbed Ezra's hand and pulled him the few feet over to the instruments. His eyes were wet with terror and he followed her gaze back to her incredulously. Shirley didn't know the plan herself but knew they couldn't wait.

She picked up the violin and handed it to Ezra, who received it with a shaking confusion. He also took the bow and gripped them both like blunt weapons. Shirley slung the tuba over herself and shook her head at him.

"No. Play," she whispered.

"What? Are you crazy? I don't know how!" Ezra tried to whisper but it came out as a panicked hiss.

The thing registered the noise and bounded to the wall.

Shirley blew into the mouthpiece. The instrument let out a sad and pitiful noise. It was a non-noise, a flatulent embarrassment.

Ezra's eyes went wide. Then, without knowing why, he positioned the violin beneath his chin and ran the bow across the strings. It was a terrible noise. A shrieking, screeching, creaking non-noise.

The beast punched through the wall and tore the paneling straight off. It roared, leaning into the space, all of its nastiness surging.

Shirley played another note. Then more. The noise howled endlessly, dissonant and disrupted. Ezra followed. The violin punctuated with violent screams. It danced around the tuba noise and they swirled into cacophony.

It was a torrent din, a tumultuous racket of pandemonium. It was the sound of a first grade band class left unattended. In the small space, the song amplified out through the opening, pushing the monster backwards.

The thing jerked, hesitating, not itself believing what was happening. The two kids witnessed the retreat and surged. They stepped forward, making still more noise, blasting their instruments for every shred of decibel.

The creature squirmed. Shirley's face was turning red. Ezra's fingers were shredding.

It cried out, then seemed to separate from itself. Two beings formed out of the one. A whole other torso, another being entirely, erupted out of its Salvador Dali jaw.

It was a man, or the body of a man, but his face was twisted in unknown agony. Long sharp fangs curled in helplessness. The black muscular arms, part his and part of the other thing, reached to his face and clawed, drawing blood.

Shirley fell to the ground in a gasp, the final breath echoing through the tuba. Ezra smashed the violin on the ground. He retained a grip on the neck, the body shattered into a jagged point, and ran at the thing screaming.

It saw him, or the vampire on top did, before he plunged the splintered wood into its chest. The object went deep as he continued to force his hand in as far as it would go. Ezra knew it was impossible yet the monster's structure seemed ameldable and pourous. It was like one of those old pin art toys, the one you make a handprint on over and over for no reason.

Vance Inescort sighed and evaporated into an explosion of dust. The rest of the creature, the ripped and sinewy parts of pale flesh and the mouthy tendrils, sludged to the ground into a pool. It bubbled and steamed as Ezra, caked in blood, backed away on his palms, having also fallen. Shirley was rolling the tuba off her and fighting to get to her feet.

The smoking pile of goo boiled and a high pitch scream sliced the air. The noise was piercing, penetrative. Ezra and Shirley covered their ears and crawled together.

Then something shot up from the remains, there was a BOOM, and a brilliant flash of color erased everything.

***

Everything was dark. Then it faded in like a fog. The scene was the same, the overturned chairs, the musical instruments strung about like weapons on a battlefield. Shirley and Ezra were face to face, on the floor in an S-shape, their bodies curved out in opposite directions.

Shirley pushed herself up, her shoulders willing themselves while her mind was still hazy. Ezra began to stir. For a split second he was afraid he wouldn't be able to move again, it felt familiar waking up like this, so he scrambled around before his muscles were ready just to prove he could.

"What happened? Did we do it? Did we win?" He was almost falling over the whole time he was standing up.

"I think so. I think you killed it." Shirley didn't seem sure. She looked around, expecting a boom or a flash. Something inexplicable to be standing there, waiting for them to notice.

"We killed it. You saved us with those instruments. What was that? How did that work?" Ezra was fruitlessly trying to wipe blood from himself.

"I don't know. It makes no sense. I was just tired of being afraid and didn't know what else to do." She scanned the room, turning full circle to see in every corner as she spoke.

"I guess it worked."

"Yeah, but you and that charging move. Like all action hero. That was amazing."

"It was pretty cool, now that you mention it," Ezra feigned to shuffle his feet bashfully.

"I didn't even know you could do that with a violin."

She took his hand and the two left the classroom. They walked through the empty halls, their arms swinging lightly in their hold; up the stairs, into the bathroom, out the window, and across the field.

The air was still and quiet. Suddenly it felt like their neighborhood, like nothing could happen. They had been here before but where they were just now wasn't here. It was another place, a place that already didn't seem real. An impossible place with impossible things that no one would believe.

Shirley and Ezra went away into the silent night, thankful for the dark, colorless sky.

THE BUCKET AND
THE WELL

1

Deep inside a pit in the earth strange creatures squirmed and mimicked the shadows. Deep in that well in the ground, so far down the sunlight never mattered, a wood bucket with a rusted handle collected drops from above. Deep, so deep that a person had never been down there, it reached into the world and rested against the guts of the planet.

Up above where existence was plain and ordinary, a field of flowers surrounded the meager structure. From there some slopes and then an upward climb, decorated with trees that cast tall shadows.

On top of the hill there was a grand house, the haunted looking kind, with large looming walls, sharp pointed spires, and big window eyes. It creaked and moaned or stood rock-silent watching, depending on the tone of the air and hue of the sky. There was a small village not far away but the path of woods and gradual steepness of the incline locked the house and well in their portal.

The Vogel Family had lived in the house since their ancestors, however many generations ago, built it. They were a large, old family, sick with traditions and plagued by disaster. Many tragedies had befell the family - illness, drownings, suicides, still-births - until whispers of a curse rose from the people in the village.

Hannah Vogel was the youngest of three sisters. Mia was two years her senior and Marie three years above her. There were also two brothers, Ben, the oldest of them all at twenty-two, and Jonas, always the baby of the Vogel house, at twelve. Although Hannah was only three years older than Jonas, their maturity could be measured in eons. Or, so Hannah thought.

She knew that in this day and age it was old-fashioned to have such a robust family. Her mother and father were classical people, seemingly from a different age. Henry had inherited the family's business earlier than anticipated with the sudden death of his father, Hannah's grandad who she never was able to meet. Henry had been just twenty-five then, the bright shining future of the family name, but with Ben at just two years old and Marie on the way, he had never imagined operating the inherited trade then. He and his wife, Melinda, had only been married for three years, somewhat in a rush to precede Ben's birth. After Marie was born, they had intended to rest for a while and repair the old house they had bought together at the center of the village.

When Liam Vogel, patriarch of the modern Vogel family, died at the innocuous age of fifty-two, a vacuum consumed the household. He was the last remaining Vogel of that generation, his own brothers and sisters already taken by the reaper that hounded the bloodline, and he left only three children of his own and his wife, Roberta.

Roberta had wed Liam in what seemed like a different world entirely, an old one of sepia tones and long lost melodies. Some suggested at the time she was using him for his family's relative wealth but they had a true bond. As the misfortunes stacked upon the Vogels over their decades together, she had been there for Liam and carved out a strong reputation for herself in civic matters that concerned this quiet corner of civilization. Yet the years wore on her health and her mind eroded, until by the time of Liam's passing she knew nothing of the man that loved her or the children that grew around her like wild things from the soil. She sat most days in her room, at the top of the house, still, quiet, and covered in shadows.

Henry was not the eldest of their sons but he was the most capable. Max, his older brother, was the only Vogel to ever depart the little hamlet of Willem. He was the fabled prodigal son, a trouble and financial burden on the family until he disappeared entirely, flailing and grasping from all that he knew. Max had left two years prior to Liam's passing and did not return for the funeral. Henry's other brother, Derek, contended with suffering both physical and mental and was only twenty at the time this void crept in on the Vogel's.

When Liam was put into the ground that spring, March of 1970, the air was still crisp and clean with the unspoiled fragrance of antiquity. In the twenty years since, Henry had operated the Vogel Funeral Home with a steady hand. His five children, Ben, Marie, Mia, Hannah, and Jonas had already outlived many who carried their name. He and Melinda were still in love and carried their burdens together. Even Roberta and Derek, the gnarled roots of the family tree, clung to life in the dim upper part of the house.

Vogel Funeral Home, a simple building that modestly held its secrets, was planted at the bottom of the hill to the house, at the edge of the village. Hannah had been there many times as a child, when there was no one to watch her or her mother needed to stop and see Henry, but less frequently as she grew older. She suspected but did not pursue the notion that this was because as she aged, she became more sensitive to what the structure was and what her family's business entailed. She had no particular desire to spend time in the walls that felt to her not unlike the coffins it housed.

Hannah preferred instead to spend her spare time, when she was not tending to schoolwork, chores, or the general dealings that arise in a crowded house of nine people, large though it was, on the grounds below the house that sprouted with flowers and greenery. The trees were tall and offered shade in which she could read her books or simply stare up at their branches as they swayed through the days and caressed the sky.

The well had been off-limits her whole life. The fear of the diminutive stack of stones, a yawning mouth into the pit of the earth, was so instilled in her from a young age that she had never even wandered to its perimeter. It sat, always just right over there, perfectly alone and patient. Deep inside, the ground changed and strange creatures squirmed. A drop fell into the bucket.

2

In 1990, Willem, PA had a population under 2,000. It was less than a small town, it was a tiny settlement, with only a few essential businesses: a barber shop simply called Barber Shop, Brinker DDS, a General Store that sold a few food and toiletry items (they also had little plastic toy soldiers that Jonas had a collection of from when he was young and accompanied Melinda to the store on monthly trips), and the Vogel Funeral Home. There was a volunteer emergency service building a little ways outside town. For anything more - including a medical doctor (Klein M.D.), comprehensive grocery shopping, and Mac Auto Repair - the drive to Glenburg was twenty minutes further, where there was also a police department, post office, and the elementary school.

The high school was yet another town over in Davenport and Melinda did not permit her children to attend. She did not approve of what she perceived to be the culture of the young people there and began homeschooling her kids when they outgrew the little brick school in Glenburg, picked like a flower that was just beginning to bloom. Melinda was well educated herself and had time to fill in her days, already spent around the dusty and secluded house, tending to Derek and Roberta.

Every morning she would drive Jonas to Glenburg Elementary. She had done this for all the children as she thought it was good for them to develop social skills and learn the basics, then return home and begin lessons for Mia and Hannah. Ben helped Henry at the funeral home. Marie talked grandly of moving away and going to college but, a couple years removed from her mother's instructions, hadn't made any attempt. Mia was in what would be her last year of education and spoke little anyway, so no one questioned her future plans. At the same time, Jonas would graduate from Glenburg Elementary and would become Hannah's junior classmate.

Hannah was a good student. The teachers at Glenburg had said so and her mom never had to fuss with her about her work. She was adept at all subjects but took a particular liking to math, with its firm rules but funny looking numbers. Her brothers and sisters thought of her as stern and studious, but Hannah often felt a whimsy within, drifting up and distracting her, imagination fluttering like flower petals in the wind.

"Hannah, are you just going to read that book all day? How long have you been out here?"

Henry shielded his eyes from the sun as he stared down at his daughter. He was of an average size, with a weathered face cupped by a grey beard. He wore glasses and covered his bald head with a grey checkered hat. He was dressed prime in black, with a vest and jacket over a white undershirt. Behind him, a floral array danced lazily in the breeze. The well stuck like a mean boulder; jagged in the bright beautiful colors.

"I don't know, I just...mom said it was reading time. She's helping Mia with math," Hannah replied.

Her brown hair splayed around her head in the grass. She had a few freckles left and hazy, blue eyes. She was lean but not as thin as her sisters, her face rounding where theirs were sharp. A long blue dress with white dots reached her ankles.

"It's late afternoon, they should be about done anyway. Let's go inside and find the plan for supper," as Henry spoke he extended his hand to Hannah, who was laying on her back in the shade, her book, *The Time Machine* by H.G. Wells, flat on her chest. "I have a feeling you were out here longer than you should have been. You usually are."

Hannah gripped his hand and, clutching her book, pulled herself to her feet. She wrapped her arm around her father's waist as they started to head towards the house.

"But I was reading. This is school work. Besides, I'm ahead in my studies anyway. Mom says I might catch up to Mia in math if she doesn't work harder."

Henry chuckled but answered in a lecturing tone. "Mia has her callings too. Maybe you could help your mom and sister instead of only getting out of their way." Catching a slump in her posture, he adds: "But yes, it is school work."

Hannah and Henry continued their climb up the hill. The trees and flowers watched them go. The sunlight, illuminating the lush greenery all around, died in the well.

3

Melinda sat with Mia at a long wooden table that filled a green sunlit room. Light streamed in through the large grid windows and settled on the old, dusty walls; washing lazily over the deep brown table to where they worked. They were positioned in the middle of the dining room, filling two of the twelve chairs that surrounded the table; framed in the center of the archway that led to the foyer.

"Okay, Mia. That is enough for now. It is time for me to go pick up Jonas."

Mia didn't respond. She sat rigidly, a tension in her shoulders, tightly gripping the pencil that hovered over erased equations.

Melinda swept some of the papers together, racked them into a pile, and slid them into a folder. Mia set the pencil down delicately, avoiding eye contact with her mother.

"It's fine, we worked hard. It's just time to go. We'll get back to it tomorrow." She rose and brushed her hand through her daughter's hair as she exited the room, opposite to the foyer, into the kitchen, a room of white tile and reflective surfaces.

Mia was still at the table when the front door clicked open and Henry entered with Hannah. He hung his keys on a hook by the door, removing his hat and placing it on the mantle. Hannah maneuvered around him and went to her sister.
"Any luck with those problems? I might be able to help if you want."

Mia said nothing but stood, pushing the chair out behind her. Her hair was darker than Hannah's, appearing almost black as it curved just above the white dress on her shoulders. The angle of her jaw was sharp and her skin was tanned. Two years older than Hannah, she was three inches shorter and was petite enough to be half her size.

She exited the room without a word, passing through the foyer to the grand staircase - ordained handrails and a red velvet carpet running down the middle. She went quickly and quietly upstairs.

"That's okay. That was nice," Henry said as he put his hands on Hannah's shoulders.

Melinda came back in, her purse over her shoulder, wearing a powder blue blazer over her white ensemble. Her hair was golden and her eyes were dark. She moved with grace and purpose. Although close to Henry in age, she looked at least a decade younger.

"I am off to get Jonas. What are you two doing?" Her voice was light, soothing.

"Nothing. Hannah offered to help Mia with her homework," Henry stated.

"Oh, I see. That was nice, Hannah. I have to go. The ribs are in the cooker. Just keep an eye on them, they should be fine."

She headed to the foyer, walking briskly.

"Is Marie with mother?" Henry followed Melinda to the door.

"Yes. She checked on Derek too. Where's Ben?"

"Finishing a few things up at work. He should be here for supper."

They pecked a kiss and Melinda left. Henry drifted to the

room on the other side of the foyer, a library like a cathedral.

Hannah stood alone at the table. She gazed down at the worn paper, thinned with restarts and rewrites, and picked up the pencil, twirling it in her fingers. The smell of food drifted in from the kitchen and the lazy afternoon felt like it would stretch on forever.

4

That night at dinner, seven of them sat in the twelve chairs, all still in their usual spots. Henry and Melinda were at either end, heads of the table. Roberta, shriveled and slouching, sat to Henry's left. Marie, beautiful and confident, sat to Melinda's right on the side close to the kitchen. Mia sat next to her and Hannah one more down, next to Roberta. The three daughters in a row, stacked by seniority like a nesting doll, and then the invisible matriarch. Jonas, boyish with curly hair, sat next to his mother, across from Marie. The two chairs next to him, for Derek and Ben, were empty.

The long table was covered with food. The succulent ribs on a platter in the middle, arranged with herbs and dashed with garlic. Plates of potatoes, green beans, corn, a basket of puffy rolls. Every person had a glass of ice water. Jonas had a stout one of milk and there were tall thin ones of Bordeaux for Henry and Melinda.

"Ben should be here soon but he won't mind if we start without him." As Henry spoke, he reached for the rolls, which were close to him.

Following his lead, every family member served themselves to whatever was nearest. Then, like the gears of some set machinery, they passed their respective dish to the next in line.

"Where's Uncle Derek?" Jonas asked brightly. He was wearing a red polo shirt with a blue collar. His bright blue eyes were as much his father's as his shining golden curls were his mother's.

"He's not going to make it tonight," Henry answered as he

spooned some mashed potatoes to his plate.

"Is he not hungry?"

"I guess not."

"Is he sick?"

"No, nothing like that. Just not hungry. Hey, you make sure you get some of those green beans."

Jonas looked caught and pulled the bowl back from his mother's hand, brushing a few of the pepper sprinkled stalks to his plate.

"So Marie, did you give any more thought to Mrs. Webster's offer?" Melinda turned to look at her as she asked.

Marie was stunning, the same golden crown of her mother's and, like Jonas, the blue eyes of Henry. Her eyes were smoky where his were bright, pooling with a mesmeric mystique. She wore flowing, silky purples that stood out sharply to the green walls.

After administering her own helping of green beans, she set her fork down and looked straight to her mother.

"Yes, I have thought about it, and I'm not going to take it."

She had barely got the words out when her mother replied: "And why not?".

"I just don't want to. I could barely stand to eat there, much less work there. I thought about it, weighed it out, and whatever meager penance I made would not be worth having to deal with the people who are always there."

Henry sighed. Melinda, fork held rigidly at attention, still hadn't even looked at her food while the other kids ate in familiar disinterest. Roberta stared at the meat and vegetables that Henry had put on her plate but had not ate anything.

"What kind of people is that?"

Marie rolled her eyes, setting her fork back down after making a half hearted attempt to pick at her ribs and move on.

"You know, townies. Basic folk, the common rabble. Whatever you want to call it."

"Marie, that is terrible. How did I raise you to be such a snob?"

"You know it's true, mother," Marie replied, again picking up her fork and poking at her food. "Mrs. Webster isn't even paying minimum wage and those kind of people don't tip. I'm going to come home every night smelling like fried fish for pennies."

Melinda seemed to boil but held it in. She stared silently at Marie for a moment, still gripping her fork. Henry finally raised his head and, chewing on a piece of meat, attempted to disrupt the swell.

"It's okay, there are still other places that might be a better fit in Glenburg. What about that new little cafe on Main Street? I heard they have great bagels."

"That place isn't going to last, dad," Marie answered cooly. "They will be closed within the year and there is no one there to tip in the meantime."

"What are you going to do then? Are you ready to start helping your father and Ben at the Home?" Melinda picked it back up as Henry returned to his meal.

"If I was going to get a lame job anywhere, it would be at one of the bars in Davenport. Tracy says she is making a hundred dollars a night on the weekends." Marie takes a bite at long last, as if to punctuate the point.

"You are absolutely not working in one of those places, or anywhere in Davenport for that matter." Melinda somewhat resignedly shifts to her plate too. "Besides, you wouldn't make as much as Tracy because you don't dress like a..."

Henry scrambled to interject: "Wow, okay. Well, keep up the search, honey. Or otherwise - your mother's right, we could always use the help at The Home if you ever want."

"Thanks, dad. I don't see the big deal anyway. It's not like it costs that much for me to live here. You have all this space anyway and I eat less in a month than Jonas does in a day." Marie sticks her tongue out at her little brother, who returns it with a big toothy grin full of celery and spices.

"The big deal is that you do something for yourself and to help this house," Melinda cuts in.

"Mom, I helped with Grandma and Uncle Derek all day. I cleaned the bathrooms and dusted the library. You couldn't pay a maid for the amount of help I do here."

There was a temporary silence, as the family considered these words and chewed on their food. Hannah glanced around the table. Mia focused on her food, Jonas looked at Marie looking at Melinda, who pretended not to notice. Henry saw Hannah watching everybody and Roberta still hadn't moved.

Then, a crash from above, a big booming sound that seemed to shake the ceiling above them. It rang through the house and echoed into a long call. Everyone looked up and stopped eating.

"What was that?" Hannah asked, as Henry rose to his feet.

"Uncle Derek probably just knocked something over. I'll go check," and he left the table.

Those remaining pretended to go back to dinner for a moment. Jonas actually did, reaching for another roll despite not being finished with what he already had. Mia had barely acknowledged any of the commotion the entire time. She was nearly as still and lifeless as Roberta.

Hannah could feel the words rising in Marie before she said them.

"Really mother, I don't mean to push it, but what are you going to do if I suddenly get a job and am away all the time? Around the house, with Derek and Grandma?"

Melinda finished chewing before she replied, taking the time to evaluate the question seriously.

"I'll have Mia. She is graduating and will have more time to help around here."

"Yeah, if she passes." Jonas shot a mean little look to Mia, who didn't even seem to notice.

"Jonas! Shame on you. I'll remember that when you need help with your homework," Melinda scolded.

Hannah finally spoke up.

"It could be good, mom. You know, having Marie and Mia help with things. That way when I go to college in a few years, you will be able to rest and not take care of everybody all the time."

Melinda smiled but shook her head.

"You're sweet, Hannah. Marie, it's not about us or money.

It's about you. Don't you want to do something more than just roam around this house all day?"

"Mom, I do a lot of stuff. Just because I'm not in school or working doesn't mean I'm not doing anything…"

As Marie went on, Hannah saw Roberta reach for her silverware. She noticed her father's empty chair and wondered how long he would be gone. The old woman stuck her fork into the plump meat. Hannah couldn't help but think her soft and wrinkled arms, with faded blue veins, looked similarly tender. She raised the steak knife to her throat.

It ripped and pulled through the skin, shredding it easier than the rib. Hannah screamed as blood erupted through the gnarled bits of flesh. Everyone flew to their feet as she pulled the knife all the way across. She fell and slumped onto the table.

The thick red fluid swam through the stew of savory foods and poured over the plate, running down the table and dripping down to the floor.

5

Ben closed the lid on his Grandmother's casket. They had disguised the wound the best they could and would be able to have the body on display at the funeral the next day. Henry had repeatedly tried to take the task from his son but Ben knew it would be harder for his father than it would be for him.

He knew that others thought him cold. Even his siblings regarded him with the kind of respect normally reserved for parents. But Ben thought he felt as deeply as anyone, perhaps only in a different way. Preparing his grandmother had been difficult but it was also an honor, a duty. Surely they couldn't take her to some other establishment in another town. And if it were to be done under their roof it should be him. That was reverence, Ben thought, and it was the last tribute he would be able to pay Roberta.

His visage mirrored his reputation. He had black hair that

he swept up into style and pale skin, fairer than anyone in the family. His dark eyes sunk in his sharp face and he dressed as his job would imply.

The old place was quiet save for his movements. It was a simple layout that served needs common to all the people who had ever dwelled there. There was a lobby with the trappings of a lounge, adjoined by an office and small storage room. The interior was understated but warm, furnished with the kind of things that felt impersonal but comforting. Then there was the chapel - or service room - brightened with flowers and candles. Behind that the preparation room, where Ben turned off the lights.

He opened the door to leave and heard the floor creak behind him. He turned and in the darkness saw someone there, a vague shape that was featureless in the inky tar air. It stood there and shook in defiance of possibility; it couldn't be there but was. The light revealed nothing, the same empty room he had attempted to leave. There was no figure or shape there, the blank empty space between him and the casket stretched out in stark barrenness. Ben caught a shiver in his throat and stifled it down as he switched off the light and left.

The air outside was cool, a fall breeze pushing leafs down the road, up the hill, summoning him home. Ben turned his collar up and, huddling for warmth, started the path.

It was a steep and winding climb to The Vogel Home from The Vogel Funeral Home. He had walked the way his entire life, from when he was young enough to hold his father's hand as they went. The thought reminded him of Roberta's hands - his grandmother's hands - so cold and pale, like they weren't even there, folded across her empty breast.

The sky was dim, not dark, but a light fog rolled over the ground. Sometimes it seemed like it was always there, lingering between the trees that spread out on either side of the road, waiting at the edge of the property like an expecting host. It had been every bit as scary as one would think for the little boy, to walk by those shaded endless woods after emerging from a place he only understood held dead people.

When Ben was twelve, Marie was ten, Mia was seven, and Hannah was five, they were playing The Scaring Game. This was one of their favorite games, they could sprawl out across the vast grounds and explore the woods as they played their macabre version of hide and seek. One of them, randomly selected, would be challenged with scaring the rest. The other three would branch out, independently, and hide in the surrounding woods. The chosen one would count a full minute and then, when the others had tucked themselves away, sneak silently off into the shadowy brush. As all of them wandered lonely through the trees, they could imagine the most horrible things waiting out there in the dark. The one chosen, the conductor, would only have to locate someone else first and start stirring their environment to make them jump. One night - it was cold, Ben remembered - Marie had scared him so bad he tripped over his own feet, landing with a mouth full of fall leaves. All she had done was step out from behind a tree. But he didn't know she was there; he would have sworn she wasn't there. He had heard strange howling and cackling in the dark for a while. He thought it was her but when she emerged symbiotically from the tree trunk - out of nowhere in the darkness and in the opposite direction from where the sounds seemed to have been - it froze his heart.

Tonight's air, chilled and whimsical, was reminiscent of that night. Ben walked alone up the sharp incline with the trees closing on either side. He thought he heard it: that same awful cackle and howl. He tried to not hear it - it couldn't be - but he hurried his steps all the same.

6

Jonas Vogel ran through the winding halls of his family home with the reckless abandon and engaged energy of a younger boy. While his friends at school had started to mature into bright or sullen teenagers, Jonas didn't behave much differently than he ever had. His mother called him "her rogue" for his harmlessly mischievous nature and fearless curiosity; those recognizing blue eyes always leering for excitement.

It wasn't that he was callous to the traumatized shadow which had suddenly curtained the household. Everyone lulled, still frozen in the headlights. There was a silent shock, an inability to express anything at all. As a rule Jonas was simply always in his head and he concluded that the best he could do for his petrified family was to be himself.

He knew that his dad, Henry, was in the living room downstairs. There with the wide windows which held back the cold grey day; taking calls, reading letters, and trying to be busy. Melinda emerged from the lounge, where her and Mia rested in dim lighting with soft records and tea, to occasionally keep him company. Marie was out; "god knows where" Melinda had said with restrained exasperation. Ben was at the funeral home, probably on his way back. Uncle Derek was unaccounted. Jonas had only seen him for a moment since the incident, in an accidental passing the day before when he emerged from his room, went straight down the stairs, and outside.

Jonas' footsteps thundered through the house, shaking the ceiling on the floor below, where Henry raised his eyes to the sound in annoyance. The main upstairs hall connected all of the bedrooms, up and down on either side of the stretch, and split off midway down to another shorter passage which met the study; a warm, oval room full of leather bound books, wood shelves, and cushioned chairs. Jonas entered, half-expecting to find his uncle, who tended to spend more time in there than anybody and could often slip unnoticed between it and his own room, the only other in the shorter hallway.

But Derek was not there. Jonas tipped on his stride and rolled his hand across the doorknob, unsure of what he was going to do even if he had found him. Now, bored already with the academic chamber, he spun back around with the inclination to go outside.

Curiously, and without explanation, the door to Derek's room suddenly stood wide open. Jonas was sure it hadn't been a moment before and didn't hear it - it was usually a noisy door. A wandering chill escaped from the room, like an outstretched finger beckoning him inside.

Jonas heeded, a trance falling on him. He walked through the open door and it closed gently behind him. There was no one else in the room.

The space was nondescript, almost sterile. There was a simple bed, a desk and chair, two tidy bookshelves, and a large black trunk. A rustic candelabrum perched on the trunk; a warm glow poured across the white wall, casting shadows in the otherwise dark room.

Jonas crossed through the monkish setting and took the candlestick in his hand, raised it up, grabbed the trunk, and lifted its lid in one unimpeded motion.

Inside there were three white gift boxes, pristine with blue bows. They sat on a large, ugly book - bound with an odd leather and what looked like human teeth. Jonas reached for the box in the middle but his eyes hardly seemed to see it. He was not there, not him; sleepwalking, possessed by actions which he did not even perceive.

The box opened to a tumor of sharp objects; a magnetic growth of nails, blades, broken glass, barbwire, and razors. Jonas didn't see it, didn't know that he plucked it out and rolled it in his hands like pizza dough until it shredded through his skin and blood flowed like marinara. With a high pitch scream he startled himself awake.

7

Uncle Derek was hanging from the big tree in the backyard. Nobody found him until they were rushing around in anticipation of the paramedics. Melinda, beside herself, sobbed and wailed as she tightly wrapped bandages around Jonas' bloody hands. Henry matched her hysteria in his own meandering, directionless way. He paced ineffectually through the lower floor rooms, waiting in the big windows for the ambulance like a siren at sea. Ben, who had stepped wearily in the door at the precise moment that Jonas started screaming, was now keeping Hannah and Mia distracted and out of the way in the lounge.

Jonas was largely despondent, staring trance-like for long stretches, then suddenly ripping into cries and whimpers that silenced his mother's. His combustible state is what caused Henry to call the ambulance as opposed to driving himself to the hospital in Rosemary, on the other side of Glenburg. He was feeling overwhelmed by the self-mutilation of his mother and son even before he saw his brother hanging effortlessly in the air by the thickest branch of their biggest tree.

The scene gripped him like a kaleidoscope, folding and spiraling, shifting and focusing in nauseating spirals. He fell to the ground, banging his knees hard against the cold floor. The scream croaked in his throat like a blown speaker.

Just then, the flashing lights of the ambulance poured through the windows and across the wall as the vehicle tugged up the final slope and parked outside the house. Henry met them in the yard, crying, screaming, leaking; tears from his eyes and drool from his lips. He writhed and raved as one of the shocked medical personnel instinctively took him in their arms.

A lament of screams and sobs twirled from the house as Melinda led Jonas to rescue, passing the portrait of Uncle Derek swinging in the backyard, framed in the window like a painting that will last forever.

Epilogue: Home of the Angels
An empty expanse of land
Swallowing itself in nameless geography
Barren, wasted, drowned
Squirming with strange creatures
Shadow insects making their own sun

Nothing to prolong them
Nothing to sustain the world around
Lifeless, consumed
Feasting, twitching in the dark
It feels like the end but something is still happening
O say does that star-spangled banner yet wave?

8

The remaining members of the Vogel Family faced each other. Melinda, head of the house, eyes stained red and never coming back. Ben dressed sharply in dark colors, a grim mask now permanently affixed to his face. Marie, who had returned with the family car as the ambulance departed, not yet knowing about Jonas or Derek, wondering briefly and stupidly why the ambulance was here if grandma was already dead. And Mia and Hannah, huddled close together, silent and downcast like scolded children.

Jonas was at the hospital. He would stay there at least overnight, possibly longer, and would likely see therapy. Henry had gone with him, riding in the back of the vehicle with his still profusely bleeding son, himself a stuttering, blubbering mess. Melinda knew he would face the authorities before returning. Uncle Derek still hung in the backyard. The police and the coroner were on the way.

Melinda felt the family fracturing, felt the whole of existence turned on its side, shook down and roughed up, unrecognizable from even the day before. A day before when her mother-in-law had already butchered herself at the kitchen table in front of her kids. Now, she faced her wilted offspring, and tried not to break.

Ben spoke first.

"Glad you could make it, Marie."

The room erupted, everyone yelled, words flew wildly. It was an indecipherable cacophony of vitriol, a chorus of chaos that she couldn't even hear as the world swirled around her and the colors of the living room blurred and merged. A timeless sickness took her and she fell to the floor.

"Look what you did!" Marie cried as she spilled to her mother, taking her in her arms.

Ben's eyes bulged. Hanna and Mia wailed ineffectually, futilely grasping each other. A parasitic cloud of misery covered them, an unseen insatiable vampiric oppressor pulled their souls up from their bodies and crashed them like lightning and thunder.

Then the house moaned. It actually physically exhaled, a deep sigh of satisfaction and putred purpose. The walls seemed to shudder and the floorboards pulsed. An odious blast gusted through the halls unsummoned.

Everything started to shake. Ben scooped his mother into his arms. Marie took the two younger girls by their hands. They huddled, a primal defense to a fear familiar deep down. Something was coming for them.

9

The back door blew open. Uncle Derek, neck crooked and broken, skin blue and cold, stepped in. The noose hung empty, dancing wantonly in the torrential weather conjuring outside in the sky and air. A flash of light, the splash of rain, his dead breath materializing like crystals in the frozen air.

The screaming continued; it had never stopped. It rose like a song, crescendoing in harmonious despair. He smiled, an evil, absent smile, and they charged to the front door, erupting out to the porch and into the yard, where red tornado clouds formed overhead.

They stumbled by the planted flowers and trimmed bushes. Ben lugged his mother but didn't feel it: pure adrenaline keeping him standing upright. Mia fell, whimpering as her knee cap hit the ground. Hannah helped her to her feet. Marie trailed behind, looking over her shoulder, up to the sky, all around in hopeless panic.

A long cylindrical tendril shot through her chest. It pillaged her organs and sent blood spraying through the air like a possessed water sprinkler. She bit down on her tongue as she collapsed to the ground, her hands slipping from that of her sisters; slipping forever into nothing.

Marie hit the ground hard and the piercing tentacle stretched back to Uncle Derek, thinning at points if necessary to be however long it needed to be. Sharp and bloody, it transfused back to his body, an unknown symbiosis in his flesh. Marie's eyes started to pool with rain, swimming in her tears, as the last breath left her body. She saw the ground; dirt turning to mud.

Hannah and Mia couldn't scream anymore. They tried but their voices had clocked out. Ben shifted his mother's weight in his arms and through his back, gazing numb at his facedown dead sister pelted by rain.

Uncle Derek appeared in the doorway and half sauntered, half shuffled across the pretty porch.

"What do you want? Who are you?" Ben's words were lost in the storm and his continued shouting fell on the deaf ears of nobody at all.

"Misery take me," he answered.

Suddenly the house cracked, sections shooting up into the air, rising as giant monolithic structures, individual and larger than reality would allow. Mammoth and jagged, piercing ever upward and surrendering the earth below.

A voice came from Uncle Derek, not his; primordial, ancient, it boomed in deep bellowing syllables forever unknown. The being evaporated into dust, upward with the glaciers of ground. The language flowed into the well and shook the bucket, spilling its contents of no consequence.

Awful idols formed in the air. Alive, winged, fanged; grimacing, grinning, making animal noises. Dozens, maybe hundreds of the impish monsters; all of a sudden everywhere.

Appeared or revealed?, Ben caught himself thinking. The

first cognate spark in a while.

The little beasts fluttered down and ripped Melinda from his arms. He fought them off but they converged, thrashing and scratching, seeming to take glee in it all. Ben, battered, took to shielding his sisters as the fiends carried their mother off into the apocalyptic horizon.

THE END

The trees twisted, the ground cracked, the air snarled; it was the end. Up above the sky erupted into maniacal laughter, ruptured in color and force, turning in circles and painting shades of every kind across everything.

Ben, Hannah, and Mia ran, hand in hand, leaping over bulbous roots and fissures without a bottom. Those demons, the fanged and horny kind, littered the air. Everywhere they flew and new monstrosities birthed from the ground, hideous and gigantic.

It was a steep downhill from the Vogel Home. That same road they walked, played, lounged on. It was much uglier. Nothing is sacred, Hannah thought. That didn't sound like her.

Ben saw Marie in the woods. Not really her, he knew, but something like her, stepping out from behind the trees. It would appear then reappear, over and over down the path, repeatedly emerging in the same exact fashion. But the other ones would stay. There was soon a forest of his dead sister, leaning out from behind the trunks with a smile that wanted to hurt him.

Mia took one last look back to what used to be their house; now fantastic - hellish spires that strained for the sky, seemingly angry at their own earthbound essence. Looking up the hill they seemed even bigger. Nothing about the scene, her home, seemed familiar. Only the well still stood.

Each girl held one of his hands and they ran in formation away from the demonic volcano. It was like everything they had ever known was severed. This alien landscape was just a mockery, salt in the wound to the last few days and the decimation of their family. What did it even matter at this point?, one of them thought.

Nothing heard and nothing watched. They sprinted, heaving, crying, yelling shouting and trying to save their breath. Everywhere everything went wrong; boulders sprung from nowhere, fire shot through the air, the ground slickened and sloped. They ran, holding tight and believing they would make it.

One of the winged creatures dove at Mia, scooping her up and fluttering away. Ben jumped, connecting a punch on its ugly face, causing Mia to fall from its grasp. Hannah softened her fall and the three fled again.

Up ahead the hill started to wane and the Vogel Funeral Home was within view. A golden checkpoint, no real refuge but somehow symbolic. It glimmered in their imagination. Behind the world turned to ash and they charged in the only direction they could.

The Vogel Funeral Home exploded into a thousand little pieces, bits of stone and glass and wood stabbing through space. There was nothing in between it and them but nothing landed. Unscathed, they watched in wonder as the ground transformed to ooze and bouquets of unholy tentacles swam over the land.

Willem, PA was overtaken by a slime of ancient hatred. The small buildings and quaint Main Street were erased from the map. Glenburg soon fell, the elementary school swimming as rafts of brick and chalkboards in the waves of evil. Davenport was swallowed, nothing left of its supposed decadence and majesty.

The three kids raced as the world collapsed. Far away, buildings started to fall and streets drowned. Before long they were nowhere that they recognized.

Up above, the hellspawn, Like flying monkeys, Mia thought, crowed and celebrated. There was a deep emptiness to the world; nothing was right.

Ben, Hannah, and Mia still held hands. They quivered, nowhere to go and nothing to strive for.

Mia spoke.

"It's okay. As long as we have each other, it will be okay."

Follow Something Spooky for more horror content from Terry Pierson.

Made in the USA
Monee, IL
06 July 2025

20566409R00049